# MAYBE IT'S A SIGN

ALSO BY E. L. SHEN

*The Comeback*

# MAYBE *It's a* SIGN

E. L. SHEN

FARRAR STRAUS GIROUX
New York

*For Dad: This is a sign that I love you*

Farrar Straus Giroux Books for Young Readers
An imprint of Macmillan Publishing Group, LLC
120 Broadway, New York, NY 10271 • mackids.com





Library of Congress Cataloging-in-Publication Data
Names: Shen, E. L., author.
Title: Maybe it's a sign / E. L. Shen.
Other titles: Maybe it is a sign
Description: First edition. | New York : Farrar Straus Giroux Books, 2024. | Audience: Ages 10–14. | Audience: Grades 4–6. | Summary: Seventh grader Freya June Sun is obsessed with Chinese superstition and signs she believes are from her late father, but an unexpected partnership with a classmate leads her on a path of self-discovery as she learns to rely on herself for luck.
Identifiers: LCCN 2023024520 | ISBN 9780374390778 (hardcover)
Subjects: CYAC: Self-actualization—Ficion. | Superstition—Fiction. | Friendship—Fiction. | Chinese Americans—Fiction. | LCGFT: Novels.
Classification: LCC PZ7.1.S51425 May 2024 | DDC [Fic]—dc23
LC record available at https://lccn.loc.gov/2023024520

First edition, 2024
Book design by Aurora Parlagreco
Printed in the United States of America by Lakeside Book Company, Harrisonburg, Virginia

ISBN 978-0-374-39077-8
1 3 5 7 9 10 8 6 4 2

# MAYBE IT'S A SIGN

# THE CONCERT

Dad always said the viola was lucky. He used to remind me every time I got sick of practicing or whined about another concert or competition. In careful detail, he reminisced about the day we first walked into the Hartswood Music Store on the corner of Eighth and Franklin—from the twinkle of the silver bell when we opened the door to Mr. Miyazaki's thin, wispy beard and wrinkly forehead as he welcomed us into his shop. For a while, my older sister, May, played the piano, so my parents thought I'd pick that instrument, too.

But no.

At first, I only cared about the decorations. The weird little busts of Beethoven and Bach and the funny crank of the music stands when you bent them backward. But at some point, I guess, I pointed at a pair of violas hanging off to the side, separate from the violins and the giant cellos. Dad was thrilled. Lucky things always came in pairs. Every good Chinese person knew that. And I had zeroed in on two violas—the instruments that would therefore make me the luckiest, would bring me the most happiness. Dad bought them both. The first was for good fortune and for my future children "who might one day want to play the viola, too" (barf). The second was, of course, for *me*. Once I curled my fingers around the pegbox and headrest, my future became clear. I was Freya June Sun: the violist.

Dad was wrong about one thing, though. I'm not lucky. Because while I still have my viola, he's been gone for eight months and five days. One afternoon in August, while I was at the kitchen table reading *The Canterbury Tales* for my summer reading assignment, Dad was at work, in some sort of accounting meeting with his coworkers. And then just seconds later, he was apparently on the floor, his heels making right angles with the blue-gray carpet. The doctors called it a massive myocardial infarction. A heart attack. I call it cosmic punishment.

Now, it's just Mom dragging May and me through the Hartswood Middle School parking lot, my patent-leather Mary Janes kicking up gravel. My viola case knocks against my dress, and I wonder if I can hit it hard enough against my thighs that I'll damage the instrument and won't have to play my solo.

"Stop doing that," Mom scolds. "We're going to be late."

"It's fine. Mr. Keating won't care."

Or more like he's given up on caring. We've been late to so many rehearsals and nearly every concert since the start of the school year. Why should my conductor expect anything different this time around?

Case in point: As we near the lobby's double doors, May putters fifteen feet behind us, rummaging through her purse. My sister hates dressing up, but tonight she has on a plaid miniskirt and a cream knit sweater. It's not because she thinks my seventh-grade spring concert is important. It's because Lucas Vanderpool will be there, watching his younger brother bang out random notes on the bass. I told her Lucas Vanderpool's face looks like a pinched rat's, and he is literally the dullest person on the planet, but May is reapplying lip gloss for him anyway. She never listens to me.

We're almost inside. I close my eyes.

*If a car honks in three seconds, it's a sign from Dad that I don't have to play.*

One thousand and one.

One thousand and two.

One thousand and three.

Silence.

*Okay, five seconds.*

Mom lunges ahead, waving us in from the doorway. May finally catches up to me, her breath hot on my shoulders. She drops her lip gloss in her bag before pulling out a white headband and stuffing it in her hair. I freeze. Choosing to wear white in your hair is like *asking* for the ancestors to smite you. You only wear it when someone's died. Dad's funeral was the first time I'd worn an eggshell ribbon in my hair. It felt like rope tightening around my scalp. When we got to the church, I was messing with it so much, it almost slipped out of my ponytail. Grandma wordlessly stopped my fiddling. I knew what she meant as soon as her fingers curled around my wrist. On that day, white *belonged* in my frizzy hair. White was for the dead.

The ribbon's still hidden in my jewelry box, beneath silk scrunchies and tchotchkes from our old summer vacations in Florida. I don't dare wear it or even look at it. But I can't throw it away, either.

"May," I say, a sudden bite in my voice, "take it off."

"Hmm?"

My sister smooths down her strands and bats her eyes under clumps of mascara. I drop my viola case on the ground.

"Seriously, May. Take it off. *Now.*"

"Don't *seriously* me. It's a headband. You'll live." She points at her sweater. "And it matches."

Before I can snap back, I hear the *click-clack* of Mom's heels as she trudges back to us, her phone waving wildly in our direction.

"Does no one see what time it is? Late. We are *late*."

I shake my head. "I'm not moving until May takes it off."

My sister scoffs. I can't believe she doesn't care. Dad taught us the rule about the color white. She always followed it when he was alive. And besides, she could wear a purple headband. Or pink. Or blue. Or, better yet, red. *That's* a lucky color. It's like she actively wants me to bomb my solo.

Our mother's eyes dart from May to me. She rubs her temples and takes long, deep breaths. We wait for her verdict.

"May," she says, "for your sister's sake, please take off the headband. You look fine without it."

"But—"

"Nope. No. End of discussion. Let's go."

With that, Mom barrels back through the double doors, and May rips off her headband, scowling. We lock eyes, and I wait for her to say it: *Dad's superstitions were ridiculous. You're ridiculous. No one cares about those silly Chinese wives' tales except you, and that's because you're immature and naive and you refuse to grow up.* But she doesn't say anything. She just stomps into the lobby.

I kneel down to pick up my viola case, its handle heavy in my palm. This whole concert is turning out to be a disaster before it's even started. Maybe *that's* a sign. Maybe I should just go back to the parking lot and hide behind the car until the whole thing is over. I shiver. Even though it's early April, the air is sweet and humid. I shouldn't be cold. The glittery polka dots on my taffeta dress feel rough under my palms. It's the same dress I wore to the winter holiday concert a year and a half ago. We played the Hallelujah Chorus from Handel's *Messiah* with the choir, and the moment the first note rang out, Dad stood up because it's supposedly a tradition going back hundreds of years, from when some British king stood for the Hallelujah Chorus at its premiere.

Dad insisted it was important to respect traditions, even though the king was long dead and he wasn't even *our* king. *I* thought it was embarrassing—Dad towering over the seated audience with his puffy hair so everyone could immediately tell we were related. I cowered behind my music stand as he bobbed his head to the squeals of the off-key choir.

Eventually, everyone else stood up, too, either because they shared some strong feelings about respecting a dead king from the 1700s or they thought he was getting an early start on giving his kid a standing ovation. By the end, you could hardly hear the out-of-tune sopranos or my many mistakes amid the crowd's premature roars and applause.

After the concert, we all got ice-cream cones from the shop down the street, and Dad bragged to my classmates' parents that he was a trendsetter. I didn't say a word. All I wanted to do was go home, bury myself under the comforter, and pretend the whole thing hadn't happened. But if I could go back in time, I'd look up from my melting vanilla cone and wrap my sticky arms around Dad's stomach and tell him: *Yes, you're a trendsetter. You're the coolest dad ever.*

I clench the taffeta in my fist and focus on the parking lot so I don't cry. There are no stragglers anymore—just rows and rows of cars under a hazy, muddy yellow sky. I am trying to remember my solo's opening notes, but all I can think of are streams of vanilla ice cream sliding down the spaces between my fingers like blood. Somewhere in the lobby, Mom is screeching my name. I stare at the sinking sun.

"Please," I whisper, "don't make me play."

Not a single car honks in response. I drop my head and stare at my feet. And then, in a reflection of my Mary Janes, I spot it. A red bird. No, two red birds. I look up and see the pair perched in a small tree on the edge of the sidewalk. Their wings are pulled tightly against their backs—bright blobs that can't be missed. As I get closer, the bigger one croaks lightly. I've never seen birds like this before. Not in Westchester, where every animal is gray or brown and boring. Not even in Orlando, where the birds are merely shadows hiding from the stifling heat. Somehow, these red birds remind me of the paper envelopes Dad slid under our plates at Chinese New Year dinners, the block of red rosin I use on my viola bow, the stories Mom and Dad used to tell over sweet jasmine tea that came in red tins. I do a mental calculation. A pair of birds, the color red. Lucky all around. Dad's finally done it. He's sent me a sign.

I step closer to the tree, and the birds dive into the air, swooping upward and skimming the school's rooftop solar panels. In an instant, they're gone. I press my viola case against my side. I know what I have to do.

# SPOTLIGHT

When I stumble through the double doors and into the rehearsal space (which is really just the middle school cafeteria), Mr. Keating breaks out in a grin so wide you'd think it was Yo-Yo Ma waltzing down the aisle instead of me, a short, nerdy seventh grader with dress sparkles stuck to her cheeks.

"Ah, Freya," he says as the entire room turns to stare at me, "just in time."

I offer an apologetic half smile as he beckons me to the piano so I can tune my instrument. I make my way over and take my instrument out of its case. Even though my back is turned, I just *know* the rest of the orchestra is glaring at me and muttering stuff like: *Oh, look, it's Freya June Sun, the girl who's never on time yet somehow always nabs the solo.* (Well, they're probably not that succinct, but you get the point.)

Stephanie Schmidt, the concertmaster, sniffs from her seat in the first row. I don't need to look at her to know she's the unofficial leader of the orchestra's glares. The solo in Senaillé's piece Allegro spiritoso is meant for either a violin or a viola. Everyone *thought* it would go to Stephanie—particularly because she's been not-so-quietly playing it during our five-minute breaks—but, no, Mr. Keating just *had* to give it to me.

Our mustachioed conductor bangs out an A, the piano note echoing against the cinder block cafeteria walls. When I squeak out my own note on the viola, the screech of my bow bounces off the ceiling. I don't know why we have to warm up in the cafeteria. Why couldn't Mr. Keating pick someplace with worse acoustics, like a janitor's closet, which could never fit forty-five people so I'd have to just sit the whole thing out? Or, better yet, why don't *I* go hide in the janitor's closet and accidentally lock myself in so I won't have to play?

I try to concentrate on tuning—twisting the pegs this way and that, slowly inhaling the smell of rosin and boy sweat and yesterday's cafeteria meatloaf. My eyes focus on my viola's deep cherrywood body until it blurs and all I can see are those two red birds in the parking lot, appearing like magic. Lucky in every way.

The last time I had luck like that, I was in fourth grade. I had to give an oral presentation on what I thought was the eighth wonder of the world for social studies. The night before, I was completely unprepared, had maybe four sentences written, and could barely remember the words *Niagara Falls* (my chosen "eighth wonder"). I thought I was going to throw up. But then Dad came into the kitchen while I was face-planting on my textbook and told me about the history of the number eight.

"It's the luckiest number," he said, "because in Mandarin, *eight* is pronounced *ba*, which sounds like *fa*. And *fa* means 'fortune.'"

"Uh-huh," I had mumbled, ignoring him in favor of permanently stamping my forehead with textbook ink.

"I'm serious," Dad insisted. Then he started rambling on and on about how the number eight is associated with success and wealth, so my presentation would *have* to go amazingly since it's on the *eighth* wonder of the world. There was no possible way I could fail or vomit or both.

I didn't believe him. But the next morning, I gave my presentation, and somehow the words flowed out of me like I had *become* Niagara Falls. I didn't stammer once. I sounded prepared and informed. My teacher gave me an A. And then directly after social studies, I found seventy-five cents on the cafeteria floor—just enough money to buy the vending machine chips I wanted. Wealth *and* success. Dad was right. Eight was lucky. Eight was magic.

He's right this time, too. It doesn't matter what I want. My father has sent me a sign. A *real* one. I have to play.

When I'm finished tuning, we file out of the cafeteria and into the hall that leads to the auditorium. We pause backstage, and my stand partner, Xena, shuffles her sheet music, the handle of her bow crushed in her fist. I'd forgotten that this is Xena's first concert at Hartswood Middle School—she just moved here from California in January. I wonder if she chose the viola because she also accidentally pointed at a pair of violas in a music store when she was six or if she had a more normal reason, like she saw a violist influencer on TikTok (if those even exist) and couldn't resist playing the most boring instrument in the world.

"You're gonna be great," I whisper. "Don't worry."

Xena brightens. "Thanks, Freya. You—"

I gently push her into the bright lights of the auditorium before she can say anything else.

Onstage, I find my seat across from Stephanie's. Even though the audience is mostly cloaked in darkness, I can still make out Mom and May in the third row, conveniently sitting behind Lucas Vanderpool and his parents, of course. My family always sits up front at concerts so they can take good pictures to send to my grandparents.

I look over to Mom's left as she leans forward to find me in the crowd of instruments and middle schoolers. There's an empty seat between her and an older lady and her grandkids. A spot for Dad. It's like he'll walk in any moment, like he's late after another work call or he stopped on the side of the road on his way here because he saw an injured animal and had to call animal control because *not* doing so would be *really* unlucky. Soon he'll fly in with his phone all charged and ready to video my Big Moment.

I glance down at my sheet music. Dad must have sent the birds because this is my first solo ever. I've never had one before. He's probably really excited in heaven. If he were actually about to walk through those auditorium doors, he'd already have my part memorized just so he could *appreciate how beautiful it was when I played it* or something cheesy like that. Except this time, I don't think I'd find it that cheesy.

Instead, as Stephanie tunes us again and Mr. Keating walks onstage to a smattering of applause, the only people I *do* see scurry in late are my best friends, Darley Banerjee and Billie Karras. We've been the tightest of trios since field day in second grade, when we all had to run the relay race together. Darley plays soccer, so she was like our team captain, peptalking us into a surprise win.

Now, she scampers just as quickly down the aisle, her long braids swinging behind her. Billie's right on Darley's tail, math homework rolled between her palms like she's about to swat a fly, a tote bag slung over her shoulder. When they get to their seats, Darley fluffs her braids and purses her lips to her phone camera. I am 100 percent sure she's Snapchatting something like *at Freya's orchestra concert!!!! Yay!!!!!* Darley loves exclamation points (and soccer) almost as much as Billie loves numbers.

While Darley fiddles with her phone, Billie immediately hunches over her problem sets, or what I assume are her problem sets since she's never *not* doing them. She tested out of middle school math, so she goes to the nearby upper school every day to take geometry with kids who are my sister's age. She finds them *so* interesting, but I think they're just mean and annoying, like May.

The orchestra stumbles through the first few pieces. I try to focus, but my eyes keep darting between Mom and her purple phone case as she takes too many photos of me, Darley Snapchatting, and Billie bent over her homework. I almost skip a measure because I can't stop internally barfing at May making googly eyes at the back of Lucas Vanderpool's head.

*Come on, Freya,* I scold myself. *Get it together. For Dad.*

In my mind, the pair of red birds have feathery wings so large they take up every corner of my brain.

I try to breathe as the audience politely claps and Mr. Keating swivels toward me on the conductor stand. We lock eyes as I raise my bow. Allegro spiritoso is starting. And it's my turn in the spotlight.

# DISASTER

"You were so great!" Mom comes up behind me, her itchy sweater rubbing against my bare arms.

"Thanks," I say, though I don't think she can hear me over the ever-growing crowd flooding the lobby with their programs and photos and praise.

My sister leans against the wall, her fingers touching the crown of her hair like she's reaching for the headband unceremoniously dumped into her purse. She must still be mad at me for making her take it off because Mom elbows her until she mumbles, "Good job, Freya," while staring across the lobby at Lucas Vanderpool's rat face.

"Thanks," I say again.

Mom beams. She's trying really hard to be peppy, I know. To make up for Dad not being here.

Anyway, they're both lying. I was not *great* or even

*good.* I sucked. I made four glaring mistakes, and I'm pretty sure Stephanie Schmidt winced when I finished.

I can't think about how I humiliated myself in a holiday concert dress for too long, though, because Darley and Billie start attacking me from all sides.

"You killed it, girl!" Darley screeches, kissing my cheek. She pulls out the program from underneath her armpit and waves it in front of my face. "Look, under Allegory Spirit-whatever, it says your name. *Freya June Sun, soloist.* I took a pic and snapped it to the entire soccer team."

"Oh, that's very sweet of you, Darley," Mom pipes up. "Did any of your teammates come to the concert?"

Darley shakes her head. "Nah," she says, "but I'm sure they will next time. Now that they know my best friend is a violin prodigy."

"*Viola.* And *not* a prodigy," I correct her. Not even close.

Billie stuffs her problem set into her tote bag. "We really enjoyed the concert," she says.

"Ya, she didn't look at her homework *once* while you were playing," Darley teases.

"Darley!" Billie swats her arm.

"For a whole five minutes! A record!"

My friends continue to play-fight each other while Mom looks at them, disturbed. My mother grew up with my Chinese immigrant grandparents, and play-fighting was *not* part of anyone's vocabulary back then. She squirms and glances toward the double doors as May examines her nails.

Outside, the sky has turned dark—squares of murky navy peeking through the lobby windows. I wonder if the red birds have returned to the parking lot or if they've given up on me and are halfway to Canada. Judging by how the concert went, they're probably in Niagara Falls at this point. It hurts to think of Dad's pained face if he were here, his disappointment at my poor playing.

"Freya!"

I turn, scanning the dozens of orchestra kids and their families packed around me until I see a hand waving in the distance. I'd recognize that hairy arm and silver watch anywhere—most days they're accompanied by a conducting baton. Mr. Keating. Probably calling me over to finally tell me the truth: I screwed up that solo. I've let him and Dad down.

Mom tucks a wayward strand of hair behind my ear. "Go talk to your conductor. We'll see you outside."

I nod and try to smile as Mom, May, Darley, and Billie fold into the horde headed for the exit. After last year's spring concert, we all went out to Happy's Drive-In—the place where the crispy chicken tenders are served on sticks with shoestring fries packed in the middle, which somehow made them yummier, more special. Darley, Billie, and I shared a table while Mom and Dad sat in the booth behind us so they could give us "privacy." We giggled about the band boys and their awkward, too-big suits. Darley stage-whispered that Aaron Pecker farted so powerfully she could hear it from the third row at the climax of the *Pirates of the Caribbean* theme song, and Billie laugh-snorted her soda all over the table. Even May was happy. She'd gotten a bunch of her upper school friends to join her at Happy's, and they'd spent the meal talking about protesting climate change or something. When May isn't crushing on dull boys, she's usually protesting *something*, and these days she won't shut up about global warming.

That night had seemed endless. We had stayed at Happy's until the world turned inky black and Mom had insisted she drive my friends home rather than wait for their parents. In the parking lot, the spring air had felt cool on our shoulders, the gravel scuffing our shoes. No one had cared that we'd be exhausted at school the next day. Not even my parents. Everything had been perfect.

Tonight, we'll all probably go home in our separate cars. Billie's mom will come to pick her and Darley up. We're definitely not going to Happy's. I haven't had chicken tenders on sticks since last summer.

I make my way through the lobby crowd, past the line

for milkshakes and other treats at the PTA-run concession stand. Stephanie's father crouches to take a photo of her against the awards case, her shiny lipstick grin matching the pink flowers on her dress.

"Smile!" he says.

But he doesn't have to tell her. She's already grinning from ear to ear.

I shuffle through a crush of parents and kids who forgot to put away their instruments so they're swinging their French horns around like expensive weapons. No one listens to me as I mumble *Excuse me* and *Sorry* and *Please, I just need to get to my conductor so he can tell me how much I suck.*

Up ahead, I spot one last obstacle before Mr. Keating: Gus Choi. Slurping a chocolate milkshake. Gus and I share one class together—Cooking & Careers—which is truly one class too many because he might be the most annoying kid on the planet. For example:

1. In first grade, he rubber-band-slingshot a crayon through the air, and it hit me in the back of the head during read-aloud time and stuck in my poofy hair and made the whole class laugh. He insisted it was an accident, but he got sent to the quiet corner to think about his actions. (As he should have.)

2. In third grade, he thought my lunchbox was his and ATE MY SANDWICH. My whole salami sandwich. *Without noticing it wasn't his.* I had to eat his chicken nuggets instead. Which were actually pretty good, but that's beside the point.

3. He *still* makes weird faces at me in the hall, and sometimes I catch him staring at me during class, even though we haven't had a real conversation since fifth grade.

Thankfully, this time, he's so intently focused on his milkshake, he doesn't see me. A lady with a giant purse almost smacks me in the head as I fight my way to my orchestra conductor. I duck, tripping over someone's feet, until I'm inches away from Gus. Just as I am about to sneak past, he notices me.

"Oh, hey, Freya!" he says. "You did—"

It happens all at once: Giant-Purse Lady knocks into his shoulder. The plastic top on Gus's milkshake cup flies off. Gus careens forward. Chocolate. Milkshake. Goes. SOARING. And the whole thing lands all over my sparkly polka-dot dress.

"Oh no." Gus whimpers. "Oh no, no, no, no, no."

I am covered in splashes of thick brown goop. It drips

down the hem of my dress onto my frilly cream socks, puddling on the floor. It 100 percent looks like someone *pooped* all over me.

"I'm really sorry!" Gus is shouting, but I can barely hear him over the sound of my own heartbeat thumping in my ears.

May's white headband *definitely* cursed me. I should have skipped this orchestra concert altogether and stayed home.

Giant-Purse Lady actually proves useful because she is now taking a million napkins out of her bag-weapon and pressing them to my dress so I look like an unfinished paper-mache piñata. I don't blink as I move past her and Gus and toward the end of the hall.

Mr. Keating is staring. Clearly, he saw the whole thing.

"Well." He gulps. "That was rather unfortunate."

I try to say something back, but all I can think about is how fitting it is that my conductor is going to say my solo was total crap while I look like literal poop.

"I'll make this quick," he says nervously, "so you can, you know . . . go home and change."

My orchestra teacher pulls out a creased piece of paper from his pants pocket. "You played wonderfully tonight, Freya, so I thought you might be great for this opportunity. It only happens once a year, and they just lowered the age group for seventh graders to audition."

I barely process his words, thinking about what Dad would have felt if he'd heard them, as my hands open and take the paper from Mr. Keating. I unfold it.

At the top, in bold letters, it reads, WESTCHESTER COUNTY ORCHESTRA COMPETITION.

"A once-in-a-lifetime opportunity," Mr. Keating insists, "and at the perfect time, too."

I peel a wrinkled, chocolate-stained napkin off my dress. *Yeah, the perfect time.*

# UNLUCKY NUMBER FOUR

It's Wednesday morning, and Darley has already come up with six different ways I can get back at Gus for spilling milkshake down my dress.

"I brainstormed all night," she gleefully announced when I slid into the bus seat next to her at the ungodly hour of 7 a.m. The sun arched over the windows, and hot vinyl pricked the backs of my legs, sticky with sweat from racing to the bus stop. For some reason, I am always running to catch the bus, even when I wake up and get ready early. May, on the other hand, rolls out of bed and does her hair and makeup in the car because her best friend, Brianna, drives her to school. Brianna could drive me, too, since the upper school campus is only a short walk away from the middle school campus, but, of course, May won't let her.

"If we're going for an eye-for-an-eye approach, you

could just *accidentally* spill orange juice on him during lunch," Darley mused.

"I don't like orange juice," I told her.

"Exactly, so you won't be sad when it's all over Gus."

Then she laughed at her joke—so loudly that the eighth graders turned to glare at us.

Now we're finishing midmorning break with Billie, our trio at last complete. Darley's arm is linked through mine and Billie is doodling comics on her iPad, when Darley gasps.

"Idea number seven!" she screeches. "You dump today's cafeteria mystery meat on him. That's even better."

Billie scrunches her nose against her stylus. "That stuff looks *and* smells like vomit."

Darley grins. "So it's perfect."

I pull at my crochet sweater so that it skims the top of my jeans. "I just want to forget about it," I mumble.

And really, I do. I know Darley is trying to help, but my best move is to ignore Gus Choi for the rest of the year and avoid future disaster. Which shouldn't be hard, considering he scampered away from me the minute our eyes met at the lockers this morning.

Besides, I have bigger problems to contend with. Like the audition form burning a hole in the bottom of my backpack. I still can't get Mr. Keating's face out of my head—his crinkled eyes, the lilt in his voice when he said *at the perfect time*. For a second, his voice sounded so much like Dad's.

The bell rings, and Billie untucks her elbow from her iPad so that we can see her screen. She flips it around to reveal this morning's doodle: a drawing of Gus with his wild hair and maniacal grin. His white shirt is *covered* in brown goop.

"An eye for an eye, right?" Billie giggles.

Darley swings her arms around our favorite artist–mathematician–future genius and squeezes her shoulders. "That's the spirit."

I roll my eyes as Darley clutches my wrist and pulls me toward Cooking & Careers. We watch Billie's ringlets and oversize backpack flounce away. *She's* headed to Enriched Language Arts—it's amazing at this point that she hasn't just skipped a grade.

When we enter Ms. Bethany's classroom, we're—as per usual—hit with an onslaught of color. It looks like a rainbow has barfed up a ton of kitchen supplies. There are multicolored whisks, spatulas, and other utensils hanging precariously from pegboards on one wall, teetering piles of stained aprons busting out of a storage closet, and dozens of neon mixing bowls strewn across the side table. The only things that *aren't* rainbow-colored are our desks and the 1970s ovens, hot plates, creaky fridges, and worktables in the back of the room.

This would all be very exciting if we actually *cooked* in Cooking & Careers. Instead, we've been learning stuff like kitchen safety and e-mail etiquette. Most recently, it's been table manners and how to build a résumé. The table manners are for important guests, like if the president rings my doorbell all of a sudden and I need to make sure he has a salad fork. The résumé is for the "careers" part of the class. According to my current draft, my "work experience" consists of babysitting my three-year-old cousin whenever she and her parents visit from San Francisco and arguing with my sister at a moment's notice. Ms. Bethany promised we'd start something new today, which is a relief because I'm about to put "knows how to fold a napkin" on my résumé just to fill the rest of the page.

I slink into my seat in the third row. My backpack thumps to the floor as I pull out my notebook. It's splattered with glitter hearts from when Darley, Billie, and I decorated our school supplies at the beginning of the semester. We were supposed to do it in September, but all my aunties stayed too long after the funeral—yelling at my mother in Mandarin, changing my sheets when they were perfectly clean, and forcing me to eat shrimp with the eyeballs attached. Now they are all back to their parts of the continent. Even the phone calls have dwindled to silence.

I trace my finger over the purple glitter heart as next to me Darley chatters to Jonnell, her soccer friend who's sitting behind her. They're talking a mile a minute about goals and strategy for an upcoming game, like they are soon-to-be World Cup champions. A stray speck of glitter trails down my notebook cover. I wish I loved the viola as much as Darley loves soccer.

The second bell rings, and Ms. Bethany finds her place at the front of the room. Her spiky pixie cut is pink this week, which must mean she's in a good mood. She dyes her hair so often, we've color-coded it. Blue is for melancholy, green is for unpredictable, and her normal coffee brown means do *not* get on her bad side.

"Ahem," she coughs, waving a rubber spatula in Gus Choi's direction. He's sitting at the end of the first row, rolling his pencil across his desktop, graphite staining its pristine surface.

He freezes. "Sorry," he says sheepishly. "I'll clean it."

I roll my eyes as he tries to erase his marks, making a different kind of mess. He's such a doofus. Maybe I *should* take Darley's advice and spill mystery meat all over him as payback.

My best friend finally stops whispering about soccer as Ms. Bethany turns to the smart board and writes slowly in digital marker. While she works, I inspect Gus's messy hair and hideous black-and-white-striped shirt. He looks like a disheveled mime. Hopefully, he'll play the part and never talk to me again.

Ms. Bethany steps aside, and we all strain our necks to look at what she's written. In big, blue letters is her description of our next assignment: THE THREE-COURSE MEAL.

Ms. Bethany smiles so widely, you can see the invisible braces lining her bottom teeth.

"I know you've all been eager to start cooking," she explains, "so I'm happy to tell you that it's finally time!"

"Okay, but a three-course meal?" Darley mutters to me, leaning over so her layered necklaces collapse onto her desk. "What does she think I am, a chef?"

As if Ms. Bethany has supersonic hearing, she stares right at Darley and says, "You're right—making a home-cooked meal is a lot of work! For this two-week project, you will be working in pairs. Together, you'll make an appetizer, main course, and dessert of your choosing to share with the class." She holds up a whisk that's been sitting on her desk. "But don't worry. We'll be practicing with our stoves and ovens and utensils so you'll have all the skills and inspiration you need ahead of your final products."

The room starts buzzing—the boys in the back are already pairing off, and I hear a voice in the front proudly announce that they make a mean chocolate lava cake. I poke Darley's shoulder.

"Partners?" I ask.

I hope she can't hear the desperation in my voice. I've never cooked. I can't even boil water. The Sun family just isn't a *home-cooked meal* kind of family. Before Dad died, we mostly ate his only staple—spaghetti and meatballs—or ordered takeout. My grandparents think it's shameful that neither of my parents can cook a proper Chinese dish, but I don't mind. Restaurant baozi taste just as good as homemade ones.

Jonnell is also staring at Darley with a look that says, *Be my partner or else.* If Jonnell and I have to wrestle for Darley's affection, I'll... Well, actually, I'll let Jonnell win. She plays soccer, so she's stronger.

The wrestling match is thankfully unnecessary because the next thing Ms. Bethany announces is that our partners will be random.

"A good opportunity for you to collaborate with new classmates," Ms. Bethany insists amid groans. "Now since we're an even class of twelve, we'll go down the rows and count off until we reach six. The second half of the class will start again from one. If you're the same number at the end of the exercise, you're partners. Understood?"

She points a painted nail at Louisa in the far-right corner. "All right, you start."

"One." Louisa says.

"Two," says the kid behind her.

"Three."

And then I realize that Ms. Bethany is looking at me. *I'm* four. The number four is as unlucky as a white headband—worse, in fact. In Mandarin, the pronunciation of *four* is almost exactly the same as the pronunciation of *death*. Elevators in China skip the fourth floor. Drivers refuse to choose the number four for their license plates. There's even a rumor that the Chinese government decided not to bid for the 2004 Olympic Games because they did not want to be cursed. I gulp. It's not like I can tell Ms. Bethany all this in the middle of a Cooking & Careers count-off.

"Four," I manage to croak.

Darley gives me a funny look, but Ms. Bethany doesn't seem to notice my distress. The count-off continues until someone says six, and the counting starts over.

"One."

*Wait.*

"Two."

*It can't be.*

"Three."

*You've got to be kidding me.*

Gus Choi wiggles his graphite-stained fingers and stares at Ms. Bethany. He grins.

"Four."

# THE COURTYARD

I have only seen Billie Karras cry three times in our five-year friendship.

The first was when she didn't place at our school's annual science fair despite making a complete light-up electrical circuit board powered by lemon and pineapple batteries as a nine-year-old. Darley and I found her in the bathroom, quietly sobbing by the hand dryers. We picked her up from the floor and got her mom to take us downtown to Colette's, our favorite place to eat in Hartswood, where we ordered her a deep-dish chocolate-chip cookie. It's what I always used to get when Mom, Dad, May, and I went to the decades-old diner, and it worked like a charm on Billie.

The second time was the summer after third grade when her dog died. He was old and had been sick for a long time. It wasn't like when Dad left us—suddenly, all at once. Still, even though Billie got a new puppy a few months later, it hurt.

The third time is now. Except Billie isn't crying because she's sad. She's crying because she's dying of *laughter*.

Our most calm and collected friend is rolling on the lush Hartswood University grass, tears in her eyes, because she cannot believe I've been paired with Gus Choi for our *two-week* Cooking & Careers project.

"It's like you're in a bad movie," she sputters between hiccups of laughter and sniffles.

Darley whips out her phone. "I'm gonna video this and post it on your birthday."

I swat her hand away. "Don't you dare."

Billie sits up, rubbing her eyes and dusting off slivers of grass and dirt from her bell-bottoms. "Come on, Freya, it's pretty funny."

I sigh, leaning back into the lawn so I'm facing the drifting April clouds. "He's terrible. And he *definitely* doesn't know how to cook."

Darley shrugs. "You never know. He might surprise you."

"Yeah, right."

The clouds seem to wink in agreement. The three of us walk the few blocks from school to the university courtyard every day after school. Well, every day I don't have orchestra rehearsal, Billie doesn't have Mathletes or Gender-Sexuality Alliance meetings, and Darley doesn't have soccer. But even before we started coming here, it's always felt like home. Mom was hired as an economics professor when I was a toddler. Growing up, I was spoon-fed stained glass windows and gothic hallways, magnolia trees in the spring, and sleds made from cafeteria trays that the students would use to slide down the science building hill when snow blanketed the campus. Back when May wasn't a horrible sixteen-year-old and was actually nice to me, we used to play hide-and-seek in the courtyard while Dad read novels by the big tree and we waited for Mom to finish up work.

I look over to that same tree, just a few yards away. It's green and flourishing, even without him there.

Darley bops up into a lunge position to stretch her hamstrings. "Moving on to more *interesting* boys," she says, "what do we think about Adrian Gray?"

I peel a windswept hair off my face and shiver. Last night's early signs of summer have disappeared, and it's back to chilly Westchester spring.

"Who's Adrian Gray?" I ask.

Darley blushes a deep pink. "An eighth grader on the boys' soccer team. He's new, and he's honestly terrible at soccer, but it's kind of cute, you know? Maybe I could teach him a thing or two."

I laugh. "You sure that's all you want to do, Darley? Just teach him *soccer*?"

Darley scrunches her nose. "Yes."

"Uh-huh." Billie snorts.

"Well, no. I don't know! Maybe!"

I sit up and wave Darley closer. "Okay, let's see pics."

Darley tumbles toward Billie and me, and we lean over her cell phone. Adrian has curly brown hair, tan skin, and a toothy grin. In one photo, his cleat hits the soccer ball, sunlight drenched over his calf like he's in an artsy advertisement for JV Soccer.

"He may not be good at playing soccer, but he *looks* good playing soccer," I say.

Darley giggles. "Right?" She swipes to the next photo. "There's this one, too. Cute, yeah?"

Adrian is playing with his puppy, a golden retriever with a striped collar and a dangling pink tongue.

"Very." I assure her.

Billie bites her bottom lip. "I'll just take the dog, please."

"Okay, but one time, we both had practice on the field, and we had break at the same time, and Adrian forgot his water bottle, so I gave him—"

And just as Darley is about to tell us all about her rom-com meet-cute with the swoony Adrian Gray, I hear my mother screeching across the courtyard.

Well, more like I hear inaudible loud noises that I could recognize anywhere as Professor Julie Sun. Which is strange because Mom hosts office hours every Wednesday from three to five thirty. It's only three fifteen.

We twist our heads toward the sound. My mom looks like an ant from here. But even so, it's clear she's dragging *another* ant-person with her. As they get closer, I examine the person's black hair, ripped shorts, and unmistakable grimace. It's my sister. And both she and Mom do *not* seem happy.

# FIGHTING WORDS

"You never want to listen to anything I have to say" is the clearest thing I can hear from the staircase landing as Mom and May fight in the kitchen below.

From my spot tucked into the corner between carpet and wall, I can see squares of tile, a sliver of kitchen counter, Mom's messy bun, and May's slicing glare.

My mother scoffs. "I listen plenty, May."

"That's not true."

"That *is* true."

"Then you should see why this is so important to me!"

Fifteen minutes ago, my mother pulled me off the courtyard grass, gave Darley and Billie a cursory, fake "Mom hello," and shoved both May and me into the minivan. At first, no one talked at all. I didn't dare ask questions, not with May staring out the window like her life depended on her extreme external focus and with Mom playing the classical music station so loudly you'd think the whole Hartswood Middle School orchestra was in the car with us (my personal nightmare, thank you).

As we reached our house, May dove out of the car, muttering something under her breath that Mom *definitely* heard, and soon they were fighting all the way from the garage to the mudroom to the kitchen.

From what I've been able to overhear, May did something bad with the upper school newspaper again. She's the layout editor, so she's the last one to see it before it goes to print. I think the advisor told her to cut a controversial op-ed, which I assumed (correctly) May herself wrote, but May didn't cut it, and lo and behold the newspaper was printed with the article, which most of the school read. Honestly, I would never tell Mom this, but I think the student body only *reads* the newspaper because they're excited for whatever drama May is dishing out this week. She may be mean and annoying, but she keeps things interesting.

"What's important is that you don't get *suspended*," Mom snaps.

True. This is May's second warning. I'm surprised she hasn't been kicked off the newspaper yet.

May throws her arms wildly into the air. I watch as silver bracelets slink down her wrists. "The Hartswood Town Council completely ignores climate change. The town's pension fund is heavily invested in fossil fuel companies. And I looked up some people on the town council. You know what? They're freaking *climate change deniers.*"

"Hartswood is invested in hundreds of companies, May. You can't encourage your classmates to go *on strike* because you disagree with some of them."

"But, like, why not? If we have *so many* investors, why should the town care about getting rid of twenty crappy ones?"

Maybe May should be a lawyer one day. She's extremely good at arguing and twisting words around to make you dizzy. Once, when she was seven and I was four, she convinced me to swap my custom-made American Girl doll and all her outfits for a handful of M&M's. They weren't even red, which would have at least made them lucky.

I watch as my mother presses her hands against her face. Long blue veins run down her arms. She seems so fragile this way, like she could break any minute. Just like Dad. I imagine him lying on the ugly office carpet, curled around a table's legs like he'd just taken a nap.

*No.* I shake my head. *Don't, Freya.*

May crosses her arms. "I'm on the newspaper for a reason," she says, her consonants stinging, "so I can effect change when those in power are abusing their positions. That's what journalism is all about. Not just to report varsity basketball scores and next week's school lunch menu."

Between the railings, I watch her hair swing. My phone lights up beside me—probably Billie and Darley asking about the drama they obviously sensed in the courtyard. Darley would never admit this to me, but sometimes she bats her eyelashes at May like the girl is Greta Thunberg or something.

Mom's shoulders are rigid, her hands moving from her face to the kitchen counter, her knuckles white.

"May," she says, voice breaking, "I just don't know what to do with you sometimes."

She turns, and I hear her slippers patter into Dad's old study. The door closes. I could never sit in there like Mom—fenced in by piles of books and magazines and framed photos from our vacations, boxes of Dad's boring accountant paperwork, May's old sheet music from before she gave up the piano, and clay teapots and other trinkets lugged back from Dad's trips to Beijing. But Mom always goes in there when May's riled her up or she's about to get emotional. The day Dad's obituary was posted, Mom sat in there for hours.

My sister sniffles before whirling around to face the staircase. I hop to my feet and dash up the last few steps, practically vaulting into my room. Maybe she won't hear me over her own pounding steps.

In my room, I stand in the dark, feeling my ribs expand and contract as I catch my breath. We're learning about trench warfare in social studies—in World War I, soldiers dug miles of giant ditches in the ground that turned into endless rat-and-mud-filled mazes topped with dirt walls they could shoot from and hide behind. May and Mom are now in their own opposing trenches. And I'm stuck in the middle, also known as no-man's-land.

When Dad used to come home from work and find a family battle going on, he always found a way into each trench, whispering to Mom and joking with May until he got her to smile, so that by bedtime, the fight was forgotten and everyone was happy again. The next morning we would all be eating his pancakes with sweet Canadian maple syrup hair and blueberry eyes and powdered sugar smiles like nothing had happened the night before. I don't know what he said to make everything better. It was like magic.

I stare up at my ceiling, which is spinning with glow-in-the-dark stars I stuck up there when I was eight. I pretend they're real stars in the sky. *Okay, Dad, send me a sign*, I silently beg. *What should I do?*

I wait one minute. And another.

Then I hear May wailing in her bedroom. Maybe that's a sign I should play peacemaker like Dad. Slowly, I find my way down the hall and knock on her door, cracked open so I can see streaks of light hit the carpet.

"May?" My voice sounds tinny and far away. "Do you . . . um . . . need a tissue or anything?"

Like Dad, I patiently wait for her response. Instead, there's some stomping, followed by the door slamming in my face. The banging reverberates against my eardrums.

"Go away, Freya," she spits.

And with that, I'm back standing in the hall, wondering if I should try to talk to Mom instead. Or surrender and go hide out in a muddy trench of my own.

# THE CHOICE

I normally despise Select Orchestra, Mr. Keating's after-school small group ensemble, especially since the pieces are harder and there are fewer instruments to cover my mistakes. But today, I don't mind it too much—and not because I've suddenly lived up to Darley's "prodigy" title but because it's shielding me from something far worse than the viola: Mom and May.

At breakfast this morning, we sat in stony silence until May dumped half her Eggo waffle unceremoniously in the trash, Mom avoided direct eye contact, and I dashed off to the bus stop.

On the bus, Darley wouldn't stop talking about Adrian. Yesterday he asked her to practice soccer after school, which is kind of cute, I guess. So I tried to lose myself in her chatter, pushing aside the memory of May's steely gaze and Mom's refusal to look up from her iPad. But now, sitting in a folding chair on the dark stage, I feel hollower than an empty orchestra pit.

Mr. Keating taps the conductor stand. "All right, let's run through that one more time. Cellos, I need you to stay on beat, okay? It's in cut time, so you should be counting. And violins . . ."

I stare out into the empty auditorium. Dad wanted me to join Select Orchestra the minute I started middle school. The day before school began, we were flipping through May's old yearbook—photos of girls with Dyson-air-wrapped curls and boys with braces holding cardboard signs that said things like THEATER CLUB and DUNGEONS & DRAGONS SOCIETY (the biggest extracurricular organization at our school, if you can believe it). Dad paused on the photo of middle schoolers holding violas and violins, jaws pressed to their chin rests, focused intently on the blurry sheet music before them. Underneath their serious photo were the words SELECT ORCHESTRA.

"Look at this, Freya," he had said, "a chance for you to shine."

Mr. Keating walks over to the cellos. They play the same measure over and over again like a robotic symphony. Xena taps my shoulder and points to the running melody dancing across our shared sheet music.

"Do you think Mr. Keating will hold auditions for the solo?" she whispers.

I shrug. "I dunno. He'll probably just give it to Stephanie."

My stand partner's eyes fall to her thighs. She wraps a loose thread on her shorts around her pinky finger. "Right," she says, "I guess that makes sense."

It takes me a second to realize that Xena's frown is so big, it might swallow her chin whole.

I pinch her sleeve. "You should go for it. Can't hurt to ask, right?"

"Really? Do you think I have a shot?"

Maybe *Xena* should have been my father's daughter instead of me. She'd never pray that Stephanie Schmidt would take her solo from her. I force my lips into a smile.

"Yeah," I say, "you're really good. Mr. Keating would be silly not to pick you."

Before I know it, the new girl's arms and bow are flinging themselves around my shoulders. "Thanks, Freya. You're the best."

I don't say anything in response. Instead, as Mr. Keating returns to the conductor stand and lifts his arms to count us in, I obediently raise my viola to play. We fly through page after page. I am a conveyer belt of notes—a smattering of sixteenth notes here, a whole note there, a mezzo forte, a decrescendo, a vibrato-y piano to finish. When I'm done, I close the sheet music and look up at my conductor. He's sighing but, thankfully, not at me.

"Cellos, you were still off," he critiques, "but that was better."

Jeez, you'd think we were practicing to perform at Carnegie Hall or something.

The clock ticks three thirty, and finally, we all start to pack up. As I'm shoving sheet music into my backpack, Mr. Keating clears his throat.

"Freya," he says, "can you hang back?"

I nod. "Uh-huh."

I mean, I'd rather feed myself to a school of piranhas, but sure, if I have to. At least I'm not covered in milk-shake poop this time.

My viola case knocks against Xena's as we weave through the empty chairs. She grins, her strawberry ear-rings jangling back and forth.

"Thanks again for your help," she says. "I'll talk to him tomorrow."

*Can she just trade places with me* now?

When I reach Mr. Keating, he is curled over the conductor stand, chewing a pencil eraser. He's in a thermal button-down today, like it's winter and not nearly the season of daffodils and trips to the city and crop tops all the girls get school warnings for even though boys can wear jeans below their literal butt cracks. *Anyway.* He smiles warmly at me—like Xena did, like we're friends.

"Freya," he begins, "how are you doing?"

I dig my sneakers into the stage. "Fine."

"Good, good." He taps the chewed pencil eraser on the stand. "I wanted to talk about the orchestra competition. Last time I mentioned it to you, you were . . . um . . . distracted." My conductor clears his throat. "Well, anyway, have you decided if you're going to audition? I'm actually seeing the competition clerk tomorrow, so if you hand the form to me now, I can give it to him for you." His voice is getting rapidly louder, like *he'll* win an award if he talks fast enough.

Well, if there's one good thing about Mom and May fighting, it's that I completely forgot about that piece of paper scrunched in the bottom of my backpack.

Mr. Keating is staring at me with big brown eyes and this expression of half eagerness, half desperation. Why can't he ask Stephanie? She would be a much better pick. Or Xena. Or literally anyone else. My grip tightens on my viola case.

"Um, I'm not sure I still have the paper," I say. "I think it's . . . Well, I—"

Mr. Keating straightens. "Oh, I can give you another form if you need it. Let's just go to my office."

"Wait, I—"

But my orchestra conductor is already scrambling down the stage steps. I struggle to catch up with him as he races out the side aisle. Great. Now I've lied *and* contributed to climate change by wasting paper. If May were here, I'd be dead meat.

The auditorium door swings behind me, and we're back in the lobby, the hall flooded with late afternoon light. I pause, staring out into the parking lot, just like that night at the concert. Soon, the after-school bus will roll in to pick me up. I have to give Mr. Keating an answer. I have to tell him something when he hands me that form.

The crumpled paper at the bottom of my backpack feels like a rock pulling me into the tile floor. I hold my breath. *Send me a sign. Send me a sign. Please, just send me a—*

At once, I see them. It's like they never left. The two red birds, pecking around on the pavement right outside, their bodies still as red as ever. One begins to chirp. I rush forward, the glass doors the only things separating us. I swear they're looking right at me.

"Dad?" I whisper.

"Freya?"

But it's just Mr. Keating, somehow beside me again, holding a brand-new, crisp application form.

"Are you okay?" he asks. His forehead wrinkles.

I swallow the lump in my throat. "Did you see that?"

Mr. Keating fiddles with the corner of the paper. "See what?"

I turn back to the glass doors, but, of course, the birds are gone. They are not meant for my orchestra conductor. They are meant for me.

"Never mind," I mumble.

I hold out my hand and take the form.

"I've decided," I tell him as his face breaks into a grin once more. "Do you have a pen?"

# WHAT'S AN AVOCADO?

At school the next day, Ms. Bethany writes in giant letters on the smart board: APPETIZERS.

Then she explains in excruciating detail what an appetizer is, like we are in second grade and not seventh. At least it's better than the speech Mr. Keating gave me yesterday, filled with advice and random tidbits about the Westchester County Orchestra Competition judges. (Fun fact: One of them will knock a point off if your posture is bad.) I'm supposed to memorize two pieces. Mr. Keating chose Bohm's Sarabande for me because he said I played it so well at the fall gala. I get to pick the other one. I might go with Debussy's "The Girl with the Flaxen Hair" just because the title is cool. It's one of Dad's favorite pieces that I've played. He was always hovering but pretending not to hover when I practiced in the living room. Sometimes he gave up and just sat on the couch across from the music stand, his hands gently sweeping through every musical pulse like he was conducting his own personal orchestra.

Ms. Bethany finishes her boring serenade on the word *appetizer* and instructs us to get into our assigned pairs.

"I have set out a couple of ingredients on the workstations behind you," she says, "and your task will be to make an appetizer out of them. This is good practice for your project, so get creative! Be *inspired*."

"Maybe this really *is Top Chef*," I mutter to Darley.

But Darley doesn't hear me. Probably because she's hunched over her notebook, writing the initials *D. B.* and *A. G.* in gel pen surrounded by purple smiley faces.

"I guess soccer practice with Adrian went well, huh?" I whisper, wiggling my eyebrows.

Darley finally looks up. Her face has literally turned into the heart eyes emoji.

"*Dude*," she says with a gasp, "it was awesome. We played soccer, and his mom made us brownies, and he has a PS5, so he showed me how to—"

"Um, Freya?"

Darley and I both turn to see Gus standing in front of us, scratching his head. When we scan the classroom, we realize everyone has already left for their workstations, whispering together as they examine their ingredients. Darley's partner, Aishu, waves at her from the back corner.

"Oh," I say, "right."

Lucky number four. Me and Gus. For the next two weeks.

Now Gus practically skips down the aisle to our workstation like he's a rabbit, his shorts flapping against his skinny thighs. A very annoying, very hyper rabbit.

"Okey dokey," he says, rubbing his hands together, "are you ready to make something awesome?"

*Why is he so chipper?*

I shrug, looping the apron draped across the wood table around my waist. "I guess so."

We survey the ingredients. There are a few slices of white bread wrapped in cellophane, mustard, tomatoes, cheese, deli turkey slices, salt and pepper, and a weird pebbly brown thing.

I peek over at Darley's workstation. She and Aishu have separated the cheese, turkey, and bread from the rest of the items.

"Great," I say, doing the same, "let's make a turkey sandwich."

Easy-peasy. It's the one thing I know how to make since I usually have it for lunch if I'm not buying. Gus nods and leans an elbow on the workstation. The sleeves of his shirt bust out of his apron—striped again because he must truly enjoy looking like a mime at school every day.

"That could work, but Ms. Bethany told us to be *creative*. And I think we could use even more of these ingredients." Gus strokes the mustard and turkey slices like they are his children. "You know, if you want."

I narrow my eyes. The last time Gus Choi handled food, he spilled it all over me. Let's also not forget the slingshot pencil debacle *and* the *stealing* and *eating* of my salami sandwich. I'd trust an actual live turkey over him.

Gus picks up the weird pebbly thing. I think it's some kind of fruit.

"We could use this," he says, "add salt, pepper, cheese, tomatoes, and maybe even turkey, though I dunno if the consistency will be right with the turkey." He juggles the brown fruit between his palms. "There are a couple of panini grills in the corner, so we can toast it."

Does he actually think we're on *Top Chef*? I point at the pebbly oval bouncing from hand to hand.

"What even is that? A kiwi?"

Gus's eyes widen. "It's an avocado, Freya."

Oh. Well, *excuse me*. It's not like I see avocados all the time. My mom does the grocery shopping, not me.

"Fine," I say, "but we're definitely adding the turkey." At least if he screws it all up, I can tell Ms. Bethany I *tried* to make a turkey sandwich.

Gus smiles. "Okey dokey."

We split up the ingredients. Gus places the avocado on a cutting board while I set out the slices of bread and the turkey packet.

I peel back the plastic on the turkey. When Dad was around, he used to do the grocery shopping instead of Mom. Not that he was a lot better at it—or at cooking. He always threw the deli turkey slices into the grocery cart because they required no real assembly—along with frozen pizzas and those suspicious-looking premade hamburger patties. He was too busy working or traveling or ferrying us to rehearsals and club meetings to cook. He cared so much about our activities. Especially May's piano and my viola. He had wanted to join an orchestra when he was our age, but his parents were too poor to buy an expensive instrument. So he gave us the opportunities he never had.

I slap the turkey onto the bread. Dad's not here, and I still have every opportunity. I think about my ballpoint signature on that audition form I handed to Mr. Keating yesterday. I think about those red birds—about Dad, telling me not to give up.

I won't. *I won't.*

"Did that turkey do something to you, Freya?" Gus jokes.

I pull at its corner, and it tears in the middle. "No," I snap.

Gus has cut the strange fruit that's apparently an avocado in half and taken out the hard, black ball in its center. He is now scoring the mushy green stuff inside with a knife he must have found in the drawer. It looks like he's making graph paper. Or maybe he wants to play tic-tac-toe?

I cross my arms. "I don't think that's right."

Gus doesn't even glance in my direction as he continues working. "Um, this is how I've always done it, but you can show me your way if you want."

How he's *always* done it? Yeah, right. Gus Choi may know what an avocado is, but he's certainly not some kind of expert. I bet Dad didn't know how to cut an avocado. I bet he also thought it was a kiwi. I bet he wouldn't look at me like Gus did with those giant, round eyes filled with a mixture of surprise, concern, and disappointment. I'd never disappointed Dad when he was alive. I'd never turned down a concert or an audition or a challenge. I won't disappoint him now.

"Yeah," I say, "I'll try."

Before I know it, I am reaching out to snatch a sliced-up avocado half from him. Our hands collide—his are smooth, not sweaty and disgusting like I thought. His grasp is firm as I yank at the weird green fruit (or is it a vegetable?).

"Wait," he says, "just give me a sec and I'll—"

He suddenly lets go. In slow motion, green cubed chunks pop free from the dark skin and go flying.

And they land.

All.

Over.

Me.

My apron. My forehead. And somehow splattered across the top of my floral shirt. I look down as a chunk rolls off my collarbone and wedges itself in my bralette.

"Not again," Gus says. His face is one out of a horror movie. "I promise it was an accident. I'm sorry, Freya. I'm so, so sorry."

A giggle cuts across the classroom. It's Darley.

"Well," she says, "Gus Choi strikes again."

# CHURCH AUNTIES

After the humiliating incident in Cooking & Careers, Ms. Bethany dabbed my shirt with water and dish soap. Except she didn't really get the stains out, so I just walked around school covered in Dawn Lemon Burst blotches mixed with light-green smears. It was decidedly *not* a fashion statement.

Darley and Billie laughed about it at our lockers later, gossiping about how clumsy Gus is and how next time I'd have to wear a hazmat suit around him or something. I giggled with them but couldn't help replaying how it had happened: Gus cutting the avocado, me pulling it from his hands, my palms on his, the way the green flecks flew over the table. If I'm being honest with myself, it *may* have been more my fault than his. I mean, I really *didn't* know what an avocado was. I still think it might be a vegetable despite what the internet says. (Yes, I googled it later.) Besides, I wasn't even thinking about Gus or vegetable-like fruits. I was thinking about that freaking audition form. I was thinking about that sign from Dad.

On the bus home, a knot of guilt stiffened in my stomach. Then Gus proceeded to spam my phone with way too many *sorry*s and crying emojis, and he became annoying again. I am seriously regretting giving him my number so we could coordinate for the project.

"Freya, pay attention."

My mother pinches my arm and brings me back to reality: a balding Chinese pastor standing in front of a very old wooden cross in a church basement, speaking in a language I barely understand.

We've been going to Chinese church ever since I was a toddler. Almost every Chinese person in Hartswood and the surrounding Westchester towns, hamlets, and villages comes here, even if they don't speak fluent Mandarin or particularly care about Jesus. It's like they silently signed a pact to become a practicing Christian when they got the keys to their new house in the suburbs.

We used to go to church every week when Dad was alive. Not that he was super into Christianity; he was more into what May calls *superstition* than religion. But Mom likes it. In fact, she likes it so much she held Dad's funeral here. It was strange and stilted—the pastor spoke entirely in Mandarin, May gave a three-sentence eulogy, I was forced to play "Amazing Grace" on the viola, and all the aunties sniffled with practiced sympathy. It didn't feel like Dad at all.

I flip to a random page in my Bible and try to push away the memory of Dad lying in a box on the stage just eight months ago. These days, we only go to church, like, once a month. I'm glad we don't go more often.

The pastor finishes up, and we start singing a hymn, this time in English, thank God (literally). It's "It Is Well," which is Mom's favorite. May tries to subtly stretch as she sings, probably because her butt is numb from sitting on these hard wooden benches. I sing very loudly to show Mom that I'm actually paying attention like she asked. But unlike all the other times we've sung this hymn at church, her mouth is not moving. When we get to *It is well, it is well with my soul*, Mom purses her lips and stares blankly at the wall behind the choir. I think about reaching out to touch her sweater but decide against it.

The second we finish, a blaring, off-tune organ plays, and we're ushered to the back of the basement, where the social committee has set up punch, tea, and cookies on a row of folding tables. The number one rule of Chinese church is that you can't leave without gossiping with every Chinese auntie. Otherwise, you might actually be struck down by God. Or lightning. One or the other.

May scoots past me, the hem of her paisley dress sweeping my knees as she makes a beeline for her two friends from school who also go to Chinese church. Even with my back turned, I can hear her giggling with them—she must be happy since Mom was too tired to ground her for the newspaper incident and the Hartswood principal said she just had to write an apology letter to the town council as punishment. Hartswood believes in holistic learning or something like that. It's one of the tenets they like to brag about on the school website.

*I'm* not let off the hook that easily. Mom grabs my wrist and drags me to the refreshments table, where women with perfect perms and black pantyhose are whispering in clusters. Even though I haven't seen them in a while, they haven't changed a bit.

There's Auntie Tsu, who brought us a disgusting tuna fish casserole the week after the funeral. We threw it away and ate cereal for dinner instead, but Mom still wrote her a thank-you note.

Auntie Sa is, as always, in a bright-pink pantsuit because she loves being the center of attention. She also loves bragging about her daughter, Emily Sa, who is apparently a seventeen-year-old art prodigy because her self-portrait was featured in *The New York Times* once.

Auntie Guo is my favorite because she regularly sneaks cookies into my pockets on our way out the door.

The other women aren't as friendly with Auntie Guo as they used to be because she divorced her husband last fall and has no kids. It doesn't matter what year it is—you don't go to Chinese church and get a divorce. It's a commandment that the aunties have basically written into their version of the Bible.

"Julie," Auntie Tsu says, "it's been a while."

My mother contorts her face into what looks like a sad clown trying to smile. "It's so nice to see you all again." She gestures to the basement doors. "I can't believe spring is almost in full swing."

"Ooh, that rhymed!" Auntie Sa interjects, gulping down her punch. "Which reminds me, a portrait by Emily of the US poet laureate was recently used for a feature in the *New Yorker*. Isn't that incredible? We just don't know what to do with that girl."

I scan the crowd for the famous Emily. She's tall and wiry, towering over the other upper school girls. I spy her in an empty pew on the other side of the basement, hunched over her phone. I wonder if she's making a masterpiece on there or just scrolling through TikToks.

Mom shifts in her skirt. "That's wonderful," she says.

"It's nothing compared to what she'll do one day," Auntie Sa replies, drumming her fingernails against her jaw. "Oh, and Emily told me all about May's... *activism*."

She says it like it's a bad word she's not sure how to pronounce.

"Oh yes." Mom laughs, her hand clenching my wrist. "May is extremely passionate about the things she cares about. I admire her integrity. And in fact, some of the alumni caught wind of May's article in the school newspaper and wrote letters thanking her for standing up against climate change."

*I'm sorry, what?* I fight the urge to choke in case I spew phlegm all over the aunties' nice church clothes. Unless I missed a pivotal conversation in the Simmering but Ongoing Fight Between Mom and May (I haven't), Mom has never openly admired my *passionate* sister's integrity. Although the part about the alumni writing letters seems true—that's probably the real reason May got let off the hook with just an apology letter.

Auntie Sa narrows her eyes. "Yes," she says, "so full of integrity, that May."

Auntie Guo must sense a war brewing between the two women because she quickly distracts my mother by handing her a cookie on a paper napkin and a cup of steaming coffee. Mom takes the offering without saying anything while Auntie Guo turns to me.

"Freya," she says, "what's new with you?"

*Oh nothing, I'm just seeing two magical red birds on a regular basis that are likely reincarnations of my dead dad.*

*And an annoying boy at school continually spills food on me. You know, the usual.*

"Not much," I say, "just school." I try to pull off a Julie Sun sad clown smile, but I think I might look like a psychopath.

"Ah, to be young and only have to think about *school,*" Auntie Tsu says with a sigh. "Those were the good old days."

Auntie Sa nods her head in sympathetic agreement while Mom stares into the depths of her coffee cup.

Auntie Tsu bobs up her head like a startled cat. "Wait," she says, "I almost forgot—you *do* have news, Freya! You're just being *humble.* Such a Sun family trait."

My mother tilts her head. "Freya has news?"

*Crap.* Auntie Tsu's son, Garrett, is in band. He plays the trombone. He must have—

"The countywide orchestra competition!" Auntie Tsu's voice is so loud, I bet May can hear it across the basement. "Garrett is also doing it for trombone. He saw Freya's name on the portal and told me. Mr. Keating only selected a few to participate, you know. What an achievement!"

*Can't anyone audition? Also, there's a portal?*

Auntie Tsu smooths down the wrinkles in her dress, her eyes darting back and forth between Mom's confused expression and my desire to melt into the linoleum floor. "Freya, you didn't tell your mother?"

I can instantly sense my mother's anger that Auntie Tsu knew something about one of her own children before she did. It's not that I didn't want to tell her. It's just that telling her would make it more *real*.

I open my mouth to respond, but Mom gets there first. "No," she says, examining my profile as I stare straight into the distance, "not until now." She's so quiet, it hurts.

Thankfully, the aunties move on since the Sun family has no more news to share. As Mom plods to the trash can to throw out her coffee cup, I glance at May, her paisley dress swishing against her ankles. She and her friends are still laughing, their hands covering their mouths like they're too astonished at their own gossip. I can't believe we used to have the same church friends when we were little.

At last, people start to trickle out into the open air, the church bell striking twelve and silencing the aunties like a welcome dismissal. Auntie Sa asks Mom if we want to join her, Uncle Sa, and Emily for dim sum at Wong's, which my mother declines, citing nonexistent "schoolwork" and "errands."

When Mom leaves me alone for a moment to collect May from her friends, Auntie Guo wraps an arm around my shoulders, her curls skimming my neck. I feel her slip cookies into my pocket.

"It's been a hard year," she whispers. "You deserve a little luck."

She drifts toward the door, and I touch my dress pocket to trace the outline of Auntie Guo's secret treats. There are two cookies in my pocket. *Of course*, that's what she meant—a lucky pair. Just like those violas I pointed at in Mr. Miyazaki's store. Just like those two red birds.

I hold her sweet good luck charms just tightly enough so they don't crumble.

# APOLOGY

Darley won't stop talking about Adrian. She's already mentioned him five times by the end of the school day. Billie and I drop by her locker, where she's pulling up her black-and-white soccer socks so the horizontal stripes stretch over her knees.

"And," she says, "he's *so* sweet and *so* nice. He's going to walk me home after practice today."

"You know what's also sweet and nice? A doughnut," Billie grumbles.

"Hardy har har." Darley slams her locker shut and leans against the door like she's staring at dreamy clouds instead of the school's beige ceiling.

I fidget with the loose straps hanging from my back-pack. The minute I woke up this morning, I had this strange feeling in my stomach, like a lead balloon had dragged my throat all the way down to my intestines. I tried to shake it off by showering, but that only made it worse. And when I got to the staircase landing, I blinked and imagined myself at the kitchen table again when Mom got The Call about my dad, her high-pitched scream into the phone receiver. The feeling couldn't be washed away by a cold swig of milk or Darley's incessant gushing about Adrian or the endless flood of equations in Ms. Callahan's algebra class.

I used to feel like this all the time when Dad first died. Sometimes I think Darley and Billie saw that my mood was particularly sour or that I wasn't talking a lot at lunch and they just refused to say anything. Eight months later, they don't even notice anymore. Or maybe I've just gotten better at hiding it.

I crouch to the floor to unzip my backpack and begin rearranging my notebooks so I don't have to look at my friends.

"Oh. My. Goddddd," Darley yelps, shoving her phone in our faces. "You guys, Adrian just asked me to get ice cream with him Friday night! *Just* us. No parents."

Billie screeches. "Darley! Friday night is *our* monthly *Forbidden Treasure* sleepover. I literally sent you a calendar invite." Of course, Billie sent us a calendar invite. Like either Darley or I use a digital calendar.

*Forbidden Treasure* is a cheesy video game the three of

us like to play. It's sort of a *Minecraft* knockoff where we have to team up to find all the secret treasure and build a civilization before our enemies get there first. Our moms used to let us play it all the time. But once we played for so long, we got migraines, and Darley threw up a bunch and had to miss school the next day. So now we're allowed one monthly all-night video game marathon and sleepover.

"Right," Darley says, biting her lip, "I forgot. Well, we can just reschedule for next Friday or something."

Billie whirls around to face me on the floor. "Freya, do you have time to rearrange your schedule so Darley can go on her date?"

Darley squeals. "Do you guys really think it's a *date*?"

"Sure." I shrug.

"'Sure' to what?" Darley asks. "The date or the rescheduling?"

"Um . . . both?"

Darley claps her cleats together in glee while Billie rolls her eyes. I could slice the tension in the air with a knife, but the shoes remind me of the black loafers Dad always wore to work, May's face when she heard the news, the cold, white hospital we drove to in a rush, the kitchen we returned home to hours later with *The Canterbury Tales* still sitting on the table—

"Freya," Darley interjects, "look who's coming. *Milk-shake boy.*"

It's Gus, books and binders tucked under his armpit, walking carefully toward us like he's afraid any sudden movement might cause some sort of food substance to fly out of nowhere and onto my clothes. I haven't talked to him since last week—Cooking & Careers is only three times a week, and Ms. Bethany was sick earlier this week, so our substitute made us watch boring videos on kitchen safety and sanitation Monday. As Gus gets closer, I almost feel bad that I let everyone think he was *entirely* to blame for the avocado-not-a-kiwi incident.

"Uh," he says, staring down at me on the floor, "hi."

"Hi, Gus," Darley replies. She sticks her cleats to her hips in an effort to appear scary, though she just looks ridiculous.

"Hi," I say.

I zip up my backpack and stand so that we're eye level. Gus isn't wearing stripes today—instead, he's got on a paint-splattered sweatshirt. I guess he looks better as a Jackson Pollock painting than a mime.

Gus cradles his binders in his elbow with his left arm, the other scratching his head. "Are you free this afternoon, Freya?"

Darley raises an eyebrow. "Free for what?"

"Yeah, free for what?" Billie echoes.

I already have one mother, I don't need *three*.

"Well, I . . ." Gus continues to stare at the floor like

I'm still crouched on the ground. "I wanted to apologize. Again. Better."

"Oh," I say.

There's something about his face that looks so open and vulnerable. It makes me think about the avocado again, about my hands yanking it away from him. The memory joins the others in the awful mental slideshow so that it's one bad Freya moment after the other, over and over again.

Darley and Billie must find apologies as uncomfortable as they find dead-Dad emotions because they're slowly slinking away.

"I have Mathletes," Billie mumbles.

"Yeah, and I have to get to practice."

Soon, it's just Gus and me in the empty hallway.

"So . . . is that a yes?" Gus asks.

I really should leave so I don't miss the bus, but I guess I have two minutes to nod and smile while Gus awkwardly apologizes. "Okay," I say, "fine."

But Gus doesn't have a speech prepared. Instead he gestures for me to follow him down the hall. "Cool," he says, "I wanna show you something."

Okay, I'm going to have to make the *after-school* bus. I wait for Gus to stop and dip into a classroom, but instead we keep moving, past the C wing and the D wing and into the J wing. (The wings aren't alphabetical—it doesn't make any sense.) I never go to the J wing. The lockers here are maroon and shiny. It's where they have electives like woodshop and technology and other things I never think about because *my* elective is orchestra. Which reminds me, I should be practicing viola right about now. I have that competition in a few weeks. I still haven't officially picked out my second piece, much less opened the sheet music.

Finally, Gus pauses in front of a door at the end of the hallway. He turns to me.

"I know I keep spilling food on you, so I thought that, um, this time I could make food for you. That you can eat. And that won't get on your shirt. Hopefully."

What is he talking about? Even if he was going to actually make me food, the Cooking & Careers classroom is in the A wing. But I don't have time to question him because Gus has already opened the door.

# COOKING CLUB

"Welcome," Gus says, "to Cooking Club."

It's like the Cooking & Careers room on steroids. There are huge wooden workbenches, even *more* rainbow-colored utensils hanging from the walls, and two shiny stainless-steel ovens built into the wall, sandwiched between a giant fridge and a row of cabinets. And there are kids.

*Everywhere.*

Jason from my math class rolling out pizza dough on a floured table. Stella and Serafina, our grade's only identical twins, making some kind of pasta dish. A crowd of classmates with pieces of fruit on long forks bent over a pot of melted chocolate. And Ms. Bethany, running around in an apron, her hair twirled up with a large, seafoam-green claw clip.

"Wow," I say, "this is kind of amazing."

"I know, right?" Gus replies, setting his backpack and binders beside a workbench. "We got the ovens in the fall, which rocked." He loops an apron over his sweatshirt and points to a stool across from him for me to sit. "We usually have guided sessions, but Ms. Bethany said we could do freestyle today. So, uh . . . is there any after-school snack you like to eat?"

Oh, he really wasn't kidding. Gus Choi is genuinely prepared to make me *a meal*. The same boy who rubber-banded me in the back of my head. And stole my salami sandwich. And sort of spilled food on me twice.

I can't think of anything. For dinner, Mom usually makes us chicken and rice, which is kind of *bleh*, or we order a pizza or pull something out of the freezer.

I scratch the back of my neck. "I don't know."

Gus drums his fists on the table. "Hmm . . . wait, I know! I'll make chicken nuggets. I've seen you eat those at lunch."

"What?" I ask. "How did you know that?"

I mean, he's right. I *do* always eat chicken nuggets at lunch. They're from the cafeteria, so they're not the best, but they're not too bad. And sometimes the crunch of the flaky skin is extra yummy.

"I usually sit at the table behind you and Billie and Darley." Gus blushes. "With Darren, Andrew, and James.

Remember, James and Billie sometimes swap fries for peanut butter cups?"

Oh yeah, they do that almost every day. I didn't realize Gus had been sitting there the whole time. I guess I haven't paid much attention to anything he does since we had class together in fifth grade.

"Yeah," I say, "I forgot."

"Anyway, *chicken time*." He briefly deflates. "But I only have chicken breasts, so we'll have to do tenders instead."

I shrug. "That's okay. I like tenders, too." I think back to the tenders on sticks at Happy's Drive-In.

Gus shoots finger guns into the air. "Okay, awesome. Let's do it."

He starts launching into a whole explanation about how he's going to use oats rather than bread crumbs for the crust and the air fryer instead of the stove since it's faster and less messy. I just nod in response.

"Okey dokey," Gus says, "please enjoy this hold music for a second."

He makes a weird robot noise before hopping from shelf to shelf, grabbing rolled oats like Mom occasionally eats before work, some green leaves from a plant on the windowsill, a bunch of spices from a wall rack, raw chicken breasts, two eggs, and Parmesan cheese from the fridge.

"Whew," he says when all the materials are gathered. "Okay, sit back, relax, and enjoy the show."

He starts confidently slicing up the chicken breasts. I can't believe Ms. Bethany lets the kids in this classroom use sharp knives. I can't believe he's not even flinching at how close the blade is to his fingers.

"Where did you learn how to do this?" I ask.

"My halmeoni taught me. She comes from Seoul to stay with us every summer."

My grandparents know how to cook, too, but they've never taught me. When they travel from the city, they usually bring preprepared food that we heat up in the oven or in the microwave. Then they dump so much fruit on our counter, we could plant a garden with the seeds.

After washing his hands, Gus preheats an air fryer next to the stove and sets up a cute mini food processor at his workstation. He pours dried oats into a tall plastic container, adding spices and salt and pepper. Then he locks the top, presses the button, pauses, and then presses it again, so the food processor sounds like a clunky motor.

"This is called pulsing," Gus says in between whirs. "You do it so the oats don't get too finely ground or the crust will lose texture."

Sure. 'Cause that explanation makes *tons* of sense. When the oats are "ground" or whatever, Gus pours them into a shallow bowl.

"Alrighty." Gus pushes the mixture to me, along with a whisk. "You wanna stir it while I add cheese?"

The last thing I stirred was brownie mix at Darley's house four months ago. But this shouldn't be too difficult, right?

"Okay," I say, and then, watching his face light up, I warn, "Though I can't promise that I won't accidentally dump the whole thing down your shirt."

Gus laughs so loudly, I can see his belly bounce underneath his apron. "That's okay, Freya," he says. "An eye for an eye, right?"

Right. Just like Darley schemed.

While I stir (so delicately I might beat a sloth for slowest movement ever) and Gus grates in cheese, we end up talking. He tells me about his halmeoni, who is half a foot shorter than him but really intimidating, *especially* in the kitchen. We laugh about Ms. Bethany's rainbow utensils and our social studies teacher's bad jokes. (We have the same teacher but not the same class period.) He asks me what I like to do after school.

"I dunno," I say. "All I do is play the viola."

I think about that competition roster sitting in a pile somewhere on a judge's desk, how if Dad were here, I'd be at home, practicing as he listened from the living room couch. He'd pick me up from school, his window rolled down, either Beethoven or old-timey Chinese classics blasting from the car speakers. I'd see the reflection of the schoolyard's trees in his glasses as he waved so energetically, girls like Stephanie Schmidt would groan: "Oh my God, Freya, your dad!" I'd give anything for him to embarrass me like that again.

"Yeah!" Gus says, bringing me back to the present as he breaks two eggs into another shallow bowl and whisks them together in the blink of an eye. Next, he dips each chicken tender into the egg mixture and then the oat mixture until it's hidden under a thick coating. "You're really good at the viola. I know I told you this at the concert, but I liked your solo a lot."

After spraying each piece with a sheen of oil, he fills a metal tray with slices of chicken while I trace a smiley face out of leftover crumbs scattered on the wooden table.

"Thanks." I rack my brain for anything else I like to do so I don't have to keep talking about orchestra. "I also like video games. Darley and Billie and I play *Forbidden Treasure* together."

Gus's head shoots up from the metal tray. "You play *Forbidden Treasure*? I love that game."

"Really?"

As Gus puts the tray in the air fryer (Ms. Bethany supervises so we don't have a middle-schooler-burns-themselves-and-has-to-go-to-the-ER incident), we gush over our favorite characters and what levels we both get stuck on. He even tells me a trick to get past the trolls on level twenty-six. I hastily type out notes on my phone.

"I'm gonna have to tell Darley and Billie next time we play," I say.

Gus beams. "Great."

After a few minutes, the fryer beeps, and Gus prances over to the machine, this time dragging me along. He pulls the drawer out to flip the pieces, and then he shows me how to turn on the light to watch them finish cooking. Finally, the machine beeps and shuts off. The chicken tenders are golden and crispy and smell like toasted cheese and garlic. He sprinkles extra Parmesan and tiny green leaves onto the chicken.

"Parsley," he helpfully explains.

"Cool, thanks." At least I know I'm not being poisoned by a random plant. Though I don't think Gus would poison me—purposefully or accidentally. I have to admit, he seems to know what he's doing in the kitchen.

Gus plates five tenders and hands them to me. "I present to you: Gus's *I am sorry* chicken tenders. And, yes, that's trademarked."

I lift one between my fingertips, still hot. When I bite into it, the crunch is delightful, the chicken expertly baked.

"Wow," I admit, "these are really, really good."

Gus shoots more finger guns at me (he is still *so* weird) while I stuff more chicken in my mouth. My cheeks are ballooning when Ms. Bethany strolls over.

"Freya? Is that you?"

"Mmmpfh." I nod while trying not to spew crumbs on my Cooking & Careers teacher.

"I made her apology tenders," Gus says proudly, "for, you know, last week's accident."

*Actually*, I want to say, *I think I was kind of at fault for that, too. So you really didn't need to make me chicken tenders. Though they are delicious. And this room is kind of cool—*

"How kind of you, Gus." Ms. Bethany shakes her head and stares into space with this wistful expression I can only call that-weird-face-adults-make-when-they're-thinking-things-you-don't-understand.

She pats my shoulder as I swallow yet another bite. "Well, welcome to Cooking Club, Freya. I hope to see you here again soon."

# THE RAINSTORM

By the time Gus and I finish talking, eating, and washing our dishes, all the other kids have left already. After Ms. Bethany locks up, Gus and I walk back through the J wing until we reach the lobby. I peer out the glass doors and realize the after-school bus is nowhere in sight. It's 4:45, far past the last pickup and drop-off.

The sky is muddy gray and blackening by the second. Gus peers up at the heavy rain clouds.

"April showers bring May flowers," he chirps in a singsongy voice.

I bite my lip to keep from laughing. I can't give him *too* much satisfaction. "It's not raining," I say.

But sure enough, droplets start to peel down the glass, and soon a steady rain pounds against the concrete.

Gus slings his backpack over his left shoulder, his binders stuffed inside, edges peeking out like armadillo spikes.

"Do you have a ride?" he asks. "My dad's coming in a few minutes. He can drive you home."

I bite my lip. How much does Gus Choi know about me anyway? Does he know my dad is dead and my mom works late? I bet he knows through the Hartswood Middle School gossip mill. I imagine his face when he heard, pity washing over it like every other awkward kid's at the funeral, this kind of syrupy, forlorn smile that says without speaking: *I am so glad this happened to you and not me.*

I blink. "Um, it's okay. I can walk home."

"Don't you live on Preston?"

He knows where I *live*, too?

"I live on Emerson," Gus explains, "so like five minutes away. Sometimes when we're driving, I see you riding your bike around the neighborhood."

Okay, either Gus Choi is a stalker or I am the most unobservant person on the planet. To be fair, my next-door neighbor, Ms. Callister, always hollers at me from her porch when I'm riding my bike because she says I'm "*zoned out, in the middle of the street, and going to get run over.*"

"Right," I say, "yeah, I do live on Preston." I calculate the distance in my head. "It's only three miles from school."

It sounds ridiculous even saying it out loud. Three miles is an approximate hour-long walk. In the pouring rain. Gus doesn't say anything, just crosses his arms. We stare out at the buckets of water pooling on the sidewalk like tiny, connecting rivers.

A black car pulls into the roundabout. Through the tinted windows, I see a man with curly hair wave. Just like Dad would if he were here picking me up.

Gus leans to the side, trying to stay balanced under the weight of his binders. "You coming? My dad doesn't allow food in the car, so I promise there won't be any more spillage."

I can't stop my lips from upturning this time. "Okay," I say, "fine."

"Great. One sec."

Gus dumps his bag unceremoniously on the floor and zips it open. His binders tumble out, skidding across the tile.

"What are you doing?" I ask.

"My friends make fun of me," Gus says, his head practically inside his backpack, "but I really hate . . . getting wet. Like, I hate pools. And beaches. Well, I don't mind sand, just the ocean part."

"What? How do you shower?"

"Oh, I just take really fast showers. Six minutes, tops."

It's a good thing I'm not standing too close to Gus

Choi because he has the potential to be *very* smelly. Two pencils roll across the floor.

"Anyway," he says, emerging from the depths of his backpack, "that's what umbrellas are for."

He holds up a polka-dot one, triumphant.

I kneel on the ground to help him restuff his pencils and binders into his backpack. "It's kind of weird that you don't like water," I tell him. "I mean, getting wet. And does that apply to water parks, too? Because water parks are—"

That's when I hear a *click* and a *pop*. I look up from Gus's backpack to see dozens of bright-blue polka dots right in my face.

Because Gus has opened his umbrella.

Inside.

This isn't even an obscure Chinese wives' tale. This is *common knowledge*. Opening an umbrella indoors is bad luck. *Very* bad luck. Dad refused to even stick his arms out the door to open one; he'd step all the way outside and subsequently get drenched to avoid any chance of the umbrella springing indoors.

My head starts to pound. This omen can only mean two things:

1. I shouldn't be hitching a ride with Gus Choi.

2. I shouldn't be with Gus Choi at all.

In other words, I shouldn't have gone to Cooking Club. I shouldn't still be at school. I should be at home, picking my competition music, practicing until my fingers are numb, making Mr. Keating proud, making Dad—

"I have to go," I blurt, jumping to my feet.

"What?"

Gus's voice is muffled from behind the umbrella. I can't look at it or him. Instead, I swerve toward the doors. They bang open, smacking into the lobby walls.

"I'm sorry," I hear myself say.

And then I'm out in the rain, soaked from head to toe. Water slides down my ankles so my socks become wet sponges, but I don't stop moving. I dart across the roundabout and into the street, my hair matted to my neck. I run until I can't hear Gus calling my name anymore.

# SECRET

I'm in a restaurant so dark, I can't see anything. I can't hear anything, either—just snippets of laughter and glasses clinking. The room is crowded. Mom and May are beside me, but they aren't really acknowledging my existence, flipping through menus and bickering with each other like I'm a ghost. Then the sirens start. They are so loud and they go on for so long, I ask, *What's going on?* but no one responds. So I rush out onto the street into a haze of flashing lights and a stretcher with a body. *Whose body?* The person's face is covered, and I'm screaming and screaming, and no one is listening—

I wake up with a start, my sheets tangled around my pajama pants like vines. When I roll over and check my phone on the nightstand, its blue light flashes 11:13 p.m.

I flop back into my pillows. It took me an hour to run

home in the rain. When I got back, Mom was out and May was holed up in her room, so I jumped in the shower and dumped my clothes in the hamper so it just looked like I was shiny and clean and not a walking, rain-soaked disaster. When Mom came back and called us down for pizza, she didn't even ask about my impromptu wet hair and pajamas. Instead, she talked about her favorite economics students—two sisters who always participate and work hard and try their best.

"That's all I want you girls to do," Mom lectured. "Try your best."

May picked at her pizza crust. "Uh-huh."

We ate the rest of our dinner in silence.

Now, I glance back at my phone. Three missed texts from Gus: *Did you make it back okay?* and then *Freya?* followed by a final *I'm kinda worried about you. You didn't drown in the rain or something, right??*

I roll my eyes. He's such a drama king. Still, I owe him an explanation. My fingers hover over the keyboard. What am I supposed to say? *Sorry I ran out, but your open umbrella freaked me out because I don't want to be cursed?*

I flip back to my other missed texts—Xena asking about our next rehearsal time, and a group chat with Darley nonstop gushing about Adrian, and Billie completely changing the subject and asking if we're *sure* next Friday will work for our *Forbidden Treasure* sleepover.

An image of Gus's worried brown eyes flickers in my mind. I write back: *Got home okay. Didn't float away, ha. See you tomorrow at school.*

Somewhere in the house, a door clicks and footsteps sound against the wood floor. Immediately, I think, *Dad?* But no, his steps were much heavier, and he always went to bed early. And besides, he's not here. He's not coming home again.

I untwist myself from my sheets and swing my legs off the bed. When I look through the gap between my bedroom door and the wall, I see a shadow tiptoeing down the staircase. Wearing heels.

"May?"

My sister freezes. In a patch of yellow light from the streetlamps peeping through the hall window, I spot her strappy wedge sandals, smooth legs, and pleated tennis skirt. She does *not* look like she's about to go to sleep.

"What are you doing?" I ask.

May holds a finger to her lips. "Be quiet," she whispers, "or Mom will hear you."

"Um, exactly. You guys *just* stopped fighting. You're kind of on thin ice. And where are you even going? It's eleven at night, May, are you—"

A soft rumble from the driveway interrupts my speech. Our heads both snap to the window.

"Is that a *car*?" I hiss.

"Look, if you don't say anything, I'll buy you another American Girl doll outfit or something."

I narrow my eyes. "I'm thirteen, May. I don't play with dolls anymore."

"Fine, I'll take you to get ice cream. You can get a medium cone."

"A *large* cone."

May sighs. "Okay, a large cone, whatever. Just don't tell Mom, okay? I have to go."

She turns toward the staircase. I watch her little heels wobble on the landing. She looks so young and tiny from here that I can't stop my thoughts from spiraling.

Who is picking her up? Is it Brianna? Is it a boy? When is she coming home? What if the person driving her doesn't know what they're doing and they hit a tree or a truck or a sign and they crash and their windshield shatters and May gets hurt and our family whittles down again from four to three to two—

"May!"

My sister whirls around, her hand clamping over my mouth before I can say anything else. "I told you to *be quiet.*"

I see her face fully now. The taupe eyeshadow. The blush dotting her cheeks. Her dark-coffee irises filled with anger and something like fear. And on the crown of her hair, a thick, white headband. The same one she wore at my spring orchestra concert. The one she knows is bad luck.

I look up at her headband and try not to picture her car slamming into the side of a truck, her body crumpled. My sister follows my gaze. With her free hand, she touches the headband and then pats my cheek.

"Don't worry," she says, her tone almost gentle. "I'll be fine."

Then she darts down the stairs and into the night.

# SUGAR COOKIES

In the morning, Mom slathers peanut butter on Eggo waffles and slides them across the kitchen table. May grabs the plate with perfect reflexes. Her knees are tucked into the crooks of her elbows, toes dangling off the chair.

"Thanks, Mom," she says cheerfully, like she didn't disappear in the middle of the night with a mysterious person in a mysterious car and return home at some unknown hour. I tried to stay awake to make sure she got back okay, but my body gave up on me, and I awoke to the sound of May brushing her teeth over the bathroom sink this morning.

Mom smiles. She must be happy that May's being polite. My sister usually doesn't come down until five minutes before Brianna picks her up—grabbing her waffle and leaving without saying goodbye. Maybe Mom thinks May is turning a new leaf. Too bad she's actually a manipulative liar.

My mother smooths down her olive pantsuit and comes to sit at the head of the table. "Did you girls get a good night's sleep?"

"Yes," May says far too quickly. We lock eyes as she gulps down a swig of orange juice. "Slept a full nine hours."

I stab my fork into a hole of peanut butter. "Yeah," I mumble, "me too."

May's face transforms into something like gratefulness, though I can't be sure. I've decided I won't rat her out—*yet*—because I don't want to listen to Mom and May argue again. Otherwise, the house might combust from their screaming.

"Good," Mom says, completely oblivious. "You'll need to be alert and chipper for when Grandma and Grandpa get here."

I almost forgot they were coming. My grandparents live in Harlem, a short thirty-minute drive from our home in Hartswood. Mom wanted them to come live near us when we settled in Westchester County, but her parents refused—noting that they've lived in Manhattan their whole lives and are "city folk at heart." So, instead, we see them at least once a month. Though they haven't been to the house since last summer. We've always driven down to the city to see them. May and I usually just sit in their gray living room and watch cable TV on their ancient television while my mother runs errands with her parents.

The longest my grandparents stayed was after Dad's funeral. They were there with the aunties and my other grandparents who live in China and barely speak English. The house felt hot and suffocating, and May listened to nonstop Taylor Swift in her room until we all begged her to come out, if only to play different music.

"How long are they here for?"

"Just through the weekend," Mom replies. "They'll pick you up from orchestra practice today, Freya, so you don't have to take the after-school bus."

She says it like it's a treat.

"Okay," I say, "thanks."

Fifteen minutes later, the morning bus rolls down the street, and I am sliding into my regular spot next to Darley. Her French braid bops like a pendulum between her backpack straps as she analyzes everything Adrian has said or texted in the past twelve hours and then asks why I didn't answer her texts last night. I give her a half-hearted excuse. Darley doesn't really care. She just keeps talking.

At least until we get to her locker and none other than Mr. Adrian Gray himself is standing there, waiting for her. *Then* she's speechless. He's just as Darley described: curly brown hair, suntanned skin, oversize soccer jersey, and baggy shorts. Darley immediately grabs his hand, and they dart down the hall.

Billie blows ringlet bangs out of her face. "Figures," she mumbles.

I play with the sole magnet stuck to the inside of my locker door—an aquamarine anchor from the last vacation we all went on as a family. Dad had always wanted to go on a cruise even though Mom thought they were gimmicky. The summer before sixth grade, she finally gave in. We took the train to New Jersey and boarded the ship there. Dad thought it was so cool that we didn't have to fly in a plane to make it to the Caribbean. The cruise had everything: a seafood bar for Dad, shopping and pool time for Mom, karaoke nights for May, and unlimited ice cream for me. On the last day, Dad paid extra so the two of us could go to a special classical music concert in the lounge. Its carpet was decorated with yellow and maroon swirls and filled with chairs occupied by old ladies in pastel-wool sweaters. Every few minutes, the women inched their seats closer together to avoid a potential draft from the ship's air-conditioning. Dad dragged me to the front row so we wouldn't miss a single wince-worthy note from the slightly out-of-tune violinist or a pluck from the glazed-over bassist. My father loved it. He sat with his back flat against the chair, mesmerized. When they played a waltz, Dad leaned forward and swayed to the beat. This time, I couldn't even be embarrassed. It wasn't like we'd see the orchestra or the old ladies in the audience again. So I let him be happy.

I pick at the magnet's corners. I haven't practiced the viola in days. What would Dad think now?

"Earth to Freya?"

Billie is waving a stack of notebooks in my face, her bangs scrambled across her forehead.

"Oops," I say. "Sorry."

She raises her eyebrows. "So? Don't you agree?" When I don't respond, she clarifies: "About Darley?"

"Um . . . yes?"

"Ugh," Billie groans, "you're both useless."

Then she, too, stalks away—probably to hang out with her GS Alliance or Mathlete friends, who are more willing to listen to her complain.

"Hey, Freya?"

*What now?* Someone else with a boyfriend or a gripe *about* boys or a person who has no idea what it's like to be thinking about your dead father on a cruise in the middle of the Atlantic Ocean while you lug your viola case back and forth from school and feel guilty for not having practiced even though you have an orchestra competition coming up—

Oh. It's Gus. Shoving a Ziploc bag into my hands.

"Do you like sugar cookies?" he asks, which is not at all how I thought he was going to start this conversation, but *okay*. "'Cause I made sugar cookies. They're break-aparts, so they're not from scratch or anything, but I had a lot leftover, so I brought you some."

I look down at the bag. Sure enough, there are two crinkly sugar cookies resting inside the plastic. I haven't had these in forever. Mom never bakes, and Darley and Billie exclusively make brownies or pop popcorn at our monthly sleepovers. I lightly press my thumb into one.

"Sure," I say, "I like sugar cookies."

Gus grins. "Awesome. Well, enjoy."

"Thanks."

He shifts back and forth from sneaker to sneaker—neon high-tops today because he is incapable of not looking like a mime or a human highlighter. I'm about to turn around and close my locker when he suddenly stares directly into my eyes through his mop of hair, a look that's coiled with concern and understanding. It's different than the one all my neighbors and classmates wore at Dad's funeral—that look of sentimental pity.

I wait for him to bring up the running-away-in-the-rain incident again, but he doesn't. Instead, he says, "Are you free this weekend? Maybe Sunday? We should probably work on our project together."

I blink away his stare and swallow the lump strangely sitting in my throat. Right, we're due to present on Wednesday.

"I can't," I tell him. "My grandparents are in town."

My mom doesn't want me to leave the house when we have guests over, even though the "guests" are my literal flesh and blood.

"Aw," he says, "too bad. Well, maybe we can work on it Monday or Tuesday."

"Sure. I'll text you."

"Cool." Gus pulls at his backpack straps. "Cool, cool, cool. Okay, bye, Freya."

"Bye."

With that, Gus scampers down the hallway. I return to my locker door and press my fingers to the blue anchor magnet. Maybe it's just too early in the morning and my brain is mush, but I'm starting to feel like it *is* too bad I can't work on the Cooking & Careers project with Gus this weekend. I think I would have liked to.

# TOO MUCH FRUIT

"Ai, Freya, you're so much taller!"

My grandmother pulls me into a lopsided hug through the passenger-seat window as I emerge from orchestra rehearsal.

"It's only been a month, Grandma. I don't think I'm *that* much taller."

To be fair, though, I haven't measured my height in a while. Mom used to make us stand against the basement wall and mark little lines in pencil with our initials and the date alongside, but she hasn't done that since Dad died.

I throw my backpack and viola on the floor so my legs are squished between the seat and the case.

My grandpa squints at me through the rearview mirror. "Your grandma's right. You'll be a giant soon. Maybe you should ride on top of the car?"

He laughs at his own joke, his fist thumping against the steering wheel.

Unlike me (apparently), my grandparents look *exactly* the same: same permed curls and dyed-black hair gelled into side parts, same sweater vests that look straight out of an L.L.Bean catalog or my mother's middle school closet.

My grandpa pulls out of the pickup circle so slowly, cars start to honk behind him. He ignores them.

"And how is our viola prodigy?" he asks.

*Why* do people insist on calling me that? Are they hallucinating when they listen to me play?

"Not a prodigy," I correct. "But fine."

"Your mother says you were asked to audition for a countywide orchestra competition," my grandmother pipes up, "that you were *handpicked* by your conductor." She says it like she's reciting something she read on a website.

"Uh-huh," I reply.

Mr. Keating tried to talk to me about that after rehearsal today, but I ran out of the auditorium before he could catch me, shouting that my grandparents were here as I sped down the aisle. Turns out, grandparents are useful excuses.

They continue chattering all the way home while I nod and say things like "sure" and "yeah" and "really cool, Grandma." When we pull into the driveway, Mom and May are waiting on the porch, May's arms crossed, a ratty sweatshirt pulled over the crop top she was wearing this morning because Mom clearly made her cover up.

I unbuckle my seat belt and stumble out of the car, my viola case stuck to my thigh like a permanent, unwanted barnacle.

"Mom, Dad!" Mom says. She and May walk down to embrace her parents after they get out of the car. For some reason, they always give May and me big hugs but are weirdly unaffectionate with their own child. May says it's a Chinese thing.

Sure enough, after embracing May, Grandma pats Mom on the shoulder like she is an obedient puppy.

"We have fruit in the trunk," Grandpa says, "so you girls can eat well."

Mom shoots May and me a look. I run inside to drop my backpack and viola case in the foyer and then come back out, dutifully following May to the trunk of their car. I inspect the scrunchie in my sister's hair. It's deep rose red. May will wear white in front of me, but never our grandparents.

May fumbles to find the latch for the trunk, her long fingernails digging under the metal lip.

"Do you want help?"

"No," May snaps. Then, softer, she mutters: "I got this."

She does, it turns out. The trunk pops open, revealing fruit. Lots and lots of fruit.

May's mouth hangs open. "Jeez. Grandma and Grandpa bought the grocery store."

I mean, she's not *wrong*. Shopping bags fill every inch of the trunk—inside them, containers of blueberries threatening to tumble onto the pavement, plums and fuzzy peaches, lychees and persimmons bulging from overstuffed paper bags, and several clusters of bananas stacked on top of each other. In the middle of the trunk lies the main event: what seem like a bajillion oranges squeezed together in flat cardboard containers.

May sighs. "We'll have to make multiple trips."

"Nah," I say, "we can do it."

Last September, when May was holed up in her room and Mom was crying a lot and the aunties were trying to stick their noses into everybody's business, I became fascinated by waiters who could carry a family of four's dishes on their forearms. I watched YouTube videos. I practiced with heavy books. So grocery bags? I'm a pro.

May raises her eyebrows as I loop shopping bag handles on each shoulder, balancing two more in one hand and a box of oranges in the other.

"Okay," she says, "weirdly, you're, like, an Olympic shopping-bag lifter or something."

I feel myself smile. This might be the nicest thing May's said to me all year.

My sister grabs a remaining bag and the last two

boxes of oranges, and we head to the front door. As we walk past, I see Grandma rummaging through her leather purse and pulling out an envelope that she's trying to stuff into her daughter's hands.

"No," Mom is saying, "that's unnecessary."

Grandpa shakes his head. "Be logical, Julie. You're a single mother. You need the money for the mortgage and the car insurance and all those other things, and we agreed to help you out. We've talked about this."

"Dad." Mom's voice is thin yet hard, pink splotches creeping up her neck. Her eyes dart toward us.

May and I immediately look away. I hustle toward the porch and walk up the creaky steps one by one. Behind me, May shuffles inside as quickly as she can. From the kitchen, Mom, Grandma, and Grandpa are still visible, huddled in the driveway, the car gleaming behind them. The window is open halfway, the screen letting in cool, early spring air. May doesn't move to close it, and neither do I. As I place the blueberries and the bananas on the counter, I listen and silently repeat the words: *single mother*. I've never heard my mom described this way. Then I replay the rest of the conversation, and a million questions run through my head. *Is Mom having trouble paying bills? Isn't she a fancy professor with a big salary? How much did Dad make as an accountant? Was it a little or a lot? How come Mom needs Grandma and Grandpa's money now?*

Even though May isn't saying a word, I can tell she's thinking similar things. We are sisters, after all. Despite the fact that she's the worst, we have ESP.

Mom is crying now, tears trickling down her cheeks and dripping onto her blouse. May comes to stand by me at the window, and we watch our weeping mother.

"Don't cry," Grandma chastises. "It's bad for you."

My sister's mouth parts. I wait for her to ask one of the questions swirling in my head or make a snide remark—or maybe a nice one for once. Instead, she gestures to the fruit.

"So," she says, "what are we going to do with four million oranges?"

# WHISPERS

Our weekend with Grandma and Grandpa is *very* boring. They make themselves right at home. We watch a lot of C-dramas and eat blueberries until our tongues turn indigo. We help Grandma and Mom mop the floor and dust the shelves, and we hold tools for Grandpa while he fixes random appliances that I'm pretty sure were not broken around the house.

At one point, May and I are forced to do a jigsaw puzzle with Grandma at the kitchen table for an hour, and we fight to stay awake. Eventually, my sister gives up and jets off with Brianna—another car in the driveway, another zoom out of the neighborhood and into the distance. I wait for Mom to be mad at May for ditching our "guests," but she doesn't say a word.

By late Sunday morning, everyone has disappeared

to their corners of the house but me. I am in the kitchen finishing my math homework very slowly, the edge of my palm smudging the paper, when I hear hushed voices in Dad's cluttered study. Grandma's "whisper" cuts through the murmurs. Her voice has always been the loudest.

"How he could be an *accountant* and mess up like this," she is saying.

I drop my pencil on the graph paper. Is she talking about Dad? And who is she talking *to*? Giving up completely on my math homework, I tiptoe to the wall across from the study, my back pressed against the plaster.

"He tried his best, Mom. No one expected him to . . ." It's my mother's voice trailing off, frayed at the edges.

"Still," Grandma says, "he should have left more for you and your girls. He should have been prepared."

As they continue whispering, I put it together bit by bit: *accountant, mess up, left more for you, prepared.* My grandmother is talking about my *dad*. She's blaming him. For not having enough money or something. For *dying*.

Tears instantly blur my vision, anger shredding my insides. I stare out the kitchen window to try to calm down, but all I can hear is my grandma's sharp, terrible whispers, my mother's resigned replies.

*Breathe, Freya, breathe.* I close my eyes and count down.

*Three.*

*Two.*

*One.*

I see them through the window the second I open my eyes. The two red birds. It's been a week or so, but they are as bloodred and as beautiful as ever. They delicately pick at the grass with their black beaks, like they are looking for something—or someone. They are looking for *me*.

"Dad," I say.

I half expect the birds to peck at the glass in response, but they stay focused on the blades of grass. Still, I have never been more grateful for a sign. The birds know what I should do.

I grab my phone and my jean jacket, slinging my backpack over my shoulder before I can change my mind. I shoot off a text to Mom and then to Gus: *You free to work on the project now?* Three bubbles appear as I stuff my feet into my sneakers. *Come on, Gus—write faster.* I am like a coach mentally yelling at her track star. *You can do it!*

Finally, an answer comes through: *Yeah! I'm around.* I am out the door and on my bike before I can even see his address, before I can hear more of what's happening in the study. I'd rather make more green mush toast than sit in this house a minute longer.

# THE GUS CHOI RANT

I park my bike in the driveway of a large, slate-gray home with navy shutters and a red door. There are a patch of daffodils by the mailbox and a tree draping its leaves over the second-floor windows. It looks like a place built for really happy people.

I shove an elastic band around my hair and wipe sweat off the nape of my neck. I've arrived in record time, biking to Gus Choi's at a speed that would win me the yellow jersey in Le Tour de France (learned about *that* in French class). But if Gus is annoyed or weirded out by my sudden appearance, he doesn't act like it. He opens the front door while I'm standing with my bike and waves from the foyer.

"Hiya, Freya!"

I feel silly waving back, but I do anyway. "Hey, Gus."

I traipse up to him, trying to push aside my sweat-pasted flyaways. Gus fist-bumps me.

"Ka-pow," he says, wiggling his fingers like our hands have made an explosion.

I roll my eyes. "Ka-pow."

The inside of Gus's house is just as nice as the outside. There's a white fuzzy carpet in the living room, a green-velvet couch, and a kitchen that's so fancy, the stove looks like it's part of the marble countertop.

"Wow," I say, "you have *two* ovens."

Gus bites his lip. "Yeah, my parents are super into cooking. That's how I learned."

*Great.* Now I feel even worse about the avocado incident. I'm basically partnered with a semiprofessional junior chef.

"Do you want to put your backpack in my room?" Gus asks.

I nod, following him up a winding wooden staircase. We walk down a plush-carpeted hallway and through a door with a plastic sign on it that says, KEEP OUT! THIS ROOM CONTAINS A TEENAGER. Gus scrunches his nose.

"My dad got that for me for my thirteenth birthday. He thinks he's really funny."

It *is* corny, but I think Dad would have liked it, too. I wonder what he would have bought for me when I turned thirteen in February.

I drop my backpack on Gus's floor. Surprisingly, his room is quite neat. His bed is made, and he has a metal grid hanging above his desk with Polaroids dangling from clothespins of him and Darren, Andrew, and James. They're skiing in one and eating pizza in another, red sauce splattered on Gus's chin. The photos make me think of Darley and Billie and all *our* ridiculous and amazing memories. We're certainly not making any now—not with Darley spending 95 percent of her time with Adrian and Billie perpetually muttering her way through the school's hallways. I shift in my socks.

"So," I say, "how should we do this?"

"Do what?"

"Uh, the cooking project?"

"Right," Gus replies, blushing. "That."

He plops onto the bed, crossing his legs under his knees. "What if we do a practice round? We can, like, come up with some ideas, get some ingredients, try it out here, and then make the real thing based on our test run."

I pick at my cuticles. "Sounds right."

"It'll be fun," he insists.

Even though he's wrong about most things, I actually believe him. Cooking with Gus *could* be fun, even though he's currently rambling about appetizers, main dishes, the merits of frozen desserts versus baked ones, and some food analogy to *Forbidden Treasure* that goes way over my head.

As his mouth moves, he gently bops up and down, his hair haloed by the glow of his bedroom lamp. It kind of looks cute like that—long and wavy like a K-pop star's. I can see why Darley likes Adrian's curls so much. Did Gus always have such good hair? And since when did he start making analogies to my favorite video game? Also, why doesn't he look like a mime or a human highlighter like usual? I must be coming down with something. Maybe all that fruit is getting to me. I'm probably—

"Ah, ladies and gentlemen, the Gus Choi rant!"

I look up to see a man who is basically a carbon copy of Gus except thirty years older. He clucks his tongue. "Are you boring our guest, mister?"

Gus blushes for the second time today. "Oh," he says, "sorry, Freya. Sometimes I get like this. If I'm going on too long, you can just—"

"No," I interrupt, smoothing out my T-shirt and collecting myself. "It's totally fine. I thought . . . I thought your ideas were great." I turn to the older version of Gus. "You must be Mr. Choi."

Gus's dad grins. "Just call me Allen. And *you* must be Freya."

He looks at us like he's observing a scene in a play. I fight the urge to pick at my cuticles again. (Mom says it's a bad habit.) Did Allen notice I was staring at Gus's hair? Why *was* I staring at Gus's hair? It's just hair, right?

Allen claps his hands together. "I hear you two chefs have a mission that I can help you complete. Ready for takeoff?"

Gus salutes his father like we're in the military even though we're just two seventh graders doing a cooking project.

"Ready for takeoff, sir."

# DO-OVER

Turns out, *takeoff* is just getting in the car, and the landing is at the supermarket a short drive away. We pull into the parking lot in the Choi family's sleek black sedan, the same one that had been idling in the pickup circle the day it poured and Gus opened his umbrella in the lobby. I hope Allen hadn't seen me race home in the rain. Otherwise, he'd think his son is friends with a weirdo.

Not that Gus and I are *friends*. We're more like partners. Acquaintances. Classmates who sometimes hang out, but only for reasons having to do with school assignments because he is *still* annoying and *did* steal my salami sandwich in third grade—

My thoughts are interrupted by the slam of a car door. Gus hops out and literally gallops his way to the grocery store. He even *neighs* for effect. I can't tell if I should laugh or be embarrassed.

Allen does neither. "Hey!" he calls after Gus, "don't slam things. This car is expensive. You break it, you buy it."

More like *you pay me back for it* since Allen's already bought the car, but I don't argue with him. Mom has taught me enough manners to not disagree with my Asian elders. If she were here, she would also insist that I call Allen "Uncle Choi" even though he told me to call him by his first name. But she isn't here. She's at home in the study, whispering with Grandma about Dad's "poor financial choices."

Allen and I amble toward the store, heading for the rows of shopping carts in the covered vestibule just outside the entrance. To my relief, Allen doesn't say anything about the rain debacle. Instead, he drums his fingers against his jean pockets.

"So, Freya," he says as I unstick a blue cart from the line of others, "do you like to cook outside of this extremely elaborate school project you're doing?"

I smirk and shake my head.

"I'm bad at cooking," I tell him. "Gus is the real chef."

Allen scoffs, unfazed. "Even if you're bad at something, you can still like it. And besides, cooking is just reading instructions. Especially baking. You know how to read, right?"

He waggles his eyebrows just like Gus, and I find myself giggling.

"Yeah," I say, "I know how to read."

"Well, good. An important life skill."

We walk into the air-conditioned store and push the shopping cart over to Gus, who is standing next to a cereal display.

"The problem," Gus mutters as he examines the rows of Cinnamon Toast Crunch and Frosted Flakes, "is that there are too many choices."

He turns around to face us, scratching his head and staring intently at the peeling paint on the walls behind the cash registers.

"You could make anything," Allen agrees, "which is why this project seems excessive. But, hey, who am I to judge your Cooking & Careers teacher?"

Gus is now pacing in front of shelves stocked with spices, completely ignoring his dad. "Should we make French food? Korean? Chinese? Indonesian? A fusion of some kind? Should we build a narrative with our dishes?"

*Build a narrative?* He's joking, right? Suddenly, my not-friend-sort-of-acquaintance grasps my shoulders. The feel of his hands against my jean jacket takes me by surprise. I try not to look at the freckles combing his cheekbones or the tendril of hair sandwiched between his eyebrows so I don't have an existential crisis in the middle of a grocery store.

"Freya," he says, "what are your favorite foods? Besides, like, chicken nuggets."

"Um, I don't know."

Gus's sneakers tap against the tile floor as he releases my shoulders.

"Ice cream?" I suggest.

"Hmm. A solid idea, but maybe a little hard to make."

"Okay," I say, "yeah."

I wish I could be more helpful. After all, it's not just Gus's project. It's mine, too. But when I think about food, all that comes to mind is the fancy Cooking Club classroom, the crunch of a hot chicken tender with oatmeal crust, Ms. Bethany's surprised smile when she saw me there. For a moment, I had forgotten about the viola. About Dad slumped on the accounting office floor. In some way, Gus distracted me with his apology. Even though I was at least 70 percent to blame for the avocado toast incident.

"Wait," I say, "what if we just do what Ms. Bethany had us do in the beginning? We look through the shelves, pick up ingredients that we like, and see what we can make out of them once we're done."

A chance for me to make up for *my* mistakes. Gus snaps his fingers.

"That's perfect! Let's split up. Dad, you stay here with the cart? We'll bring things to you."

"Aye, aye, captain."

Gus races off to the produce shelves, a blur amid the colorful displays of fruits and vegetables. To make it seem like I know what I'm doing, I confidently walk into a random aisle, past a mother toting her baby in the front section of her cart. Once I'm alone, I stop and stare . . . at shelf after shelf stacked with all different kinds of flour and sugar along with rows of frosting, sprinkles, and chocolate—so much chocolate. Ah. The baking aisle.

I've only ever baked brownies out of a box, and that was about four months ago with Darley and Billie. Plus, Darley did most of the work. I just poured in the oil.

I've always had a thing for sweets. Sometimes, Dad would take us out and treat us to dim sum and egg tarts after church service, the crumbly pastries melting on our tongues. We bit into thick mooncakes at Mid-Autumn Festival and crunchy hup toh soh during Lunar New Year celebrations. Grandma and Grandpa always hand May and me steaming red-bean buns when we visit them in the city. Grandpa insists he makes the insides from scratch, but I once saw the H-Mart plastic bag and bean-paste container in the trash. No one has ever taught me a family recipe or how to inexplicably eyeball a bunch of measurements and make some dish magically taste good.

I don't know how to cook any of these family classics. I am Freya June Sun, the violist, *not* the chef.

I crouch down to the bottom row filled with bags of chocolate chips, running my fingers along the bags' serrated edges. Dad didn't like making dessert, but he did love eating it. One of our last meals together was supper at Colette's Diner. Mom, Dad, May, and I scrunched into a blue-vinyl booth, the threat of sunset drifting overhead. It was the middle of summer, when daylight lasted forever, and Mom was on school break, and Dad often drove us to the Catskills where we swam in nippy, gray lakes and dried off on sandy porches. May and Mom were in "a period of peace," as Dad liked to say. Basically, they hadn't fought in two weeks.

As we ate our burgers and grilled cheeses at Colette's, I snuggled under Dad's armpit, the feel of his grasp solid and reassuring. At the end of the meal, Dad declared he was stuffed. Yet when the server asked us if we wanted to see a dessert menu, he immediately said, "Yes!" We all got a laugh out of that. Even May was smiling, her stomach shaking underneath her shirt. What was it that Dad got for dessert again?

As I try to remember, my fingers hover over a bag of dark-chocolate chips. Of course—I can't believe I almost forgot. I snag the chocolate chips like a tiger snatching its prey and quickly google a recipe on my cell phone. *Aha.* For once in my life, I know exactly what I want to do.

# DEEP-DISH

"And for our main course, an herb-butter roast chicken."

If you told me two weeks ago that I'd be sitting at Gus Choi's dinner table as he balanced an enormous, crispy, golden chicken on an antique silver tray, I would have laughed you out of the room. But here I am in a plush dining room chair seated between Allen and Marcy, Gus's mom, who has straight black hair, a small, round face, and the nicest smile I've ever seen.

"Wow, kid," Allen says, "I have to say... This is a masterpiece."

It really is. Gus should come over and cook *my* family Thanksgiving dinner. Maybe I can hire him.

After Allen drove us home from the grocery store, Gus and I got to work. For appetizers, we used Gus's cucumbers and a bit of ground beef to make oyi namul, which is one of Gus's favorite snacks. They're basically stir-fried cucumbers, and they're delicious. I let Gus lead the way and just did some of the stirring and measuring and cleaning up. And I barely did anything on the roast chicken—that was all Gus's work.

But I actually loved making our dessert—Dad's favorite diner food—a deep-dish chocolate chip cookie. I found a recipe online with a photo that looked *exactly* like the one we had at Colette's and did exactly what Allen told me to do: read the instructions.

In Gus's kitchen, I preheated the oven and softened the butter in the microwave, and then Gus showed me how to use their fancy stand mixer. I got lost in the whir of the machine as it blended together the white and brown sugars, eggs, softened butter, maple syrup, and vanilla extract (which smelled so good I was tempted to taste it). Then I added in the flour and other dry ingredients. The mixer's hum was calming, like white noise or when Mom falls asleep to Netflix and the voices from the television jumble in the background. Folding in the chocolate chips. Scooping out the cookie dough. Pressing the batter into the greased skillet. Sliding it into the oven.

Baking my dessert became a lullaby.

Is this how the bakers at Colette's Diner feel every time they make a deep-dish chocolate chip cookie? Like the whole world has gone silent? Like it's just them and the dough?

Gus cuts into a piece of roast chicken and chews rapidly. "It's good," he agrees, "but it needs something."

"I think it's perfect," Marcy says gently.

"No such thing as perfect, only great." Gus replies like it's a family saying or a bumper sticker. I almost snort. Tell that to my grandparents.

But Marcy just chuckles in response. "Touché."

I examine the chicken on my plate, surrounded by a pool of brown sauce and herbs.

"Rice," I say suddenly. "It needs rice."

Gus wags a finger in the air. "Rice! That's perfect. We can put some steamed white rice in tiny bowls, Asian style, with chopsticks and soy sauce. A French-Asian fusion." At that, he mashes his fists together. "Ka-pow."

I grin. *Ka-pow*, indeed. The rest of the dinner goes fantastically. I fill up on cucumbers and chicken and giggle at Allen's bad stories and Marcy's quiet but sly jabs. When I look up from my plate, I catch Gus staring at me—and not in a creepy way. In kind of a good way. My throat clenches, and I gulp down my water.

When I bring out my deep-dish chocolate chip cookie, Gus's parents *ooh* and *ahh*. The recipe said to add a layer of chocolate chips on top before putting the skillet in the oven, but I decided to ditch my very important *reading skills* and try something new. I asked Gus how to melt chocolate in the microwave, and he told me to do it in twenty- to thirty-second increments or else the chocolate would burn. When the liquid turned deep brown and sloshy, I drizzled it over the top of the cookie. Now, it looks like I'm a *real* baker.

When everyone has scraped their plates clean, Gus's dad pats his tummy.

"Well," he says, "Freya, Gus, that was a fantastic test run." He pretends to hand out pieces of paper. "A-pluses for you both."

I wait for the wave of pride to hit me. I did it. I made a perfect deep-dish chocolate chip cookie. And I liked making it. I liked *eating* it. (It was a pretty excellent cookie, if I do say so myself.) I'm excited to bake again with Gus next week.

But right now, as Allen tosses out mock grades and Marcy brushes hair out of her son's face and Gus licks the back of his spoon, I don't feel pride. I don't feel anything except a sinking weight in my gut, like I am the *Titanic* hitting an iceberg before dropping to the bottom of the ocean.

This is all just temporary. I am not in Gus's happy family, in his very happy house, perpetually making happy food. Mom and Dad won't ever beam over me like this at the dinner table. When I get home, the Sun family storm cloud will continue to hang. Mom and May will probably start fighting again, and Grandma will still be saying horrible things about Dad. The viola will wait for me in the corner, begging me to practice.

The red birds, the grocery store, the cooking and baking—they haven't changed a thing.

# CAUGHT

I bike home as the sun begins to set and the sky paints itself pastel pink. As I pedal, I think about Grandma and Grandpa's sixty-five oranges on the counter. Maybe I can learn how to make orange cake or orange bread, if that's a thing. I'll have to look it up later.

When I arrive, our house looks quiet, my grandparents' car untouched, like no one has gone anywhere since this morning. I key in the garage door code and squish my bike next to Mom's car. In the mudroom, I kick off my sneakers and tiptoe through the kitchen and into the foyer. The hall is pitch-black, so I flick on the lights, only to see Mom waiting for me on the staircase like a creepy ghost.

"Oh my God!" I shout. "You scared me."

"Don't take God's name in vain," Mom snaps, her arms crossed. "Where were you? It's almost dark."

"I know," I say, backing up against the coatrack. Mom hasn't looked at me like this in years—her cutting eyes, lips flat and pruned. I hold on to a winter puffer sleeve as if it's somehow going to save me from her wrath. "I was—"

"I expect this from your sister," she steamrolls. "That girl is always out somewhere. But not *you*. You should have called or at least texted—"

"I did text! I texted you as soon as I left."

"No, you didn't."

"I *did*. Please, Mom, just check."

Her eyes narrow even more, but she begrudgingly yanks out her phone from her back pocket and scrolls through her messages. I watch her face in the harsh blue light of the iPhone. I know when she sees my proof: She droops and then mellows.

"There are a few," I say, just in case she's too angry to notice them all. "I was at Gus Choi's for a school project. He lives, like, five minutes away. We have a big project for Cooking & Careers that we have to work on together. I texted when I left and when we went to the grocery store and when we started cooking and right before I got home. I figured you saw them and were . . ." I hesitate. "Busy."

At that, my mother looks up from the phone. Now that she's not about to eat me for supper, I spot the puffy bags under her eyes, the redness at the corners. She's been crying. About Dad? About what Grandma said? I am too afraid to ask.

"I'm sorry," I say on default, "I should have asked for permission." I know she was worried. Mom already has one daughter who's never here. Who *sneaks out* in the middle of the night.

Mom sighs. Her flimsy slippers patter down the stairs toward me.

"Okay, Freya," she says, which is not exactly an admission of guilt, but I'll take it. "Just tell me where you're going next time. To my face. Especially when your grandparents are here. They're *guests*, you know."

Guests who talk badly about Dad behind my back? I bite my tongue, and my lips pucker at a twinge of blood.

"Of course," I say, "I promise. I actually have to go back to Gus's tomorrow or Tuesday after school to finish the cooking project. If that's all right."

I wince in preparation for her to snap again. But the next thing my mother does surprises me. Her hand reaches out to touch my face. Her fingers stretch across my ear, and I lift my chin to fold my cheek into her palm. For some reason, I want to cry.

"Yes," she whispers, "that's fine."

Then she releases her hand and traipses back up the stairs, me behind her, like her duckling or her shadow.

# PRESENTATION DAY

Grandma and Grandpa head home Monday, packing into their car some leftover fruit (they took back a bag of plums and half the oranges, phew) and their overnight bags. On my way to the school bus, I kiss Grandma's cheek, and she pats my head and says, *Don't you worry, little girl*, which is weird because how does she know I'm worrying? And what is she referring to exactly? There are so many things to worry about.

Like our Cooking & Careers presentation. On Wednesday morning, Allen drops Gus off in the circle. I meet him in the lobby, and we shuffle to the Cooking & Careers classroom loaded with food. Gus's backpack clinks with sauce bottles and Tupperware as he balances a large foil tray filled with precut roast chicken in his arms. Meanwhile, I'm juggling the appetizer containers and my hopefully delicious dessert squished into a cast-iron skillet (courtesy of Gus's house, of course) and covered by layers and layers of cellophane. We make our way to the classroom to slide our food into the industrial fridge for our presentation in class later.

Gus rambles the whole way there, which doesn't really bother me—I've gotten used to it by now. Besides, I'm too busy focusing on making sure my deep-dish chocolate chip cookie doesn't break.

Yesterday at Gus's, I made my dessert for the second time. Even though I had the recipe saved on my phone, I realized I didn't need it anymore. Unlike with my sheet music (I can *never* remember my viola pieces by heart), I saw the words melding in my mind like warm, sweet butter and melty chocolate. I already knew the ingredients, the measurements, every step to the recipe.

Gus was humming and cooking his own thing, but I wasn't listening. I was hearing my own melody: the buzz of the microwave, the whoosh of the sugar into the bowl, the plop of the batter onto the skillet. It was like I was conducting my own personal orchestra.

When I finished baking, I decided the cookie needed a little something extra, something the recipe *didn't* suggest: a touch of salt to go against all that sweetness. I thought I would sprinkle the top at the last second before serving. I mentioned it to Gus, and he thought it was a great idea. He loaned me the big box of coarse sea salt from their pantry, which is now lurching around in my backpack, matching the feeling in my belly.

Gus, on the other hand, doesn't seem the least bit nervous. "So the washing machine broke, but it's okay because this shirt really isn't that dirty," he rambles as we totter down the hallway. "Mom sprayed Febreze on it and said it was fine."

I glance at his T-shirt pinned against the big foil tray. It's striped again, though this time with rainbow colors. Looks like he's a *neon* mime today. It's kind of cute. Cheery, even. As we file into the A wing, he wrinkles his nose, freckles scrunching together.

"It doesn't smell, right?"

"No, Gus, your shirt doesn't smell." I tighten my grip on the container handles so the skillet doesn't slide off its top. "And worse comes to worse, you can always rub some of that tinfoil on yourself and then you'll just smell like chicken."

Gus laughs and then starts coughing, and then he's laughing some more, so hard his face turns red. It's addictive, and I find myself laughing, too, my mouth spread wide even though it was a bad joke.

"Okay," a high-pitched voice squeals, "plot twist."

I look over to see Darley and Adrian leaning against their lockers, his arm draped around her shoulders. She's wearing her hair in two French braids with satin ribbons at the ends, painted stripes swiped across her cheeks. I forgot she had a soccer game today. I guess we haven't talked in a bit.

"We're presenting," I explain, holding up my container, "for Cooking & Careers today."

Darley twists a braid around her finger. She disentangles from Adrian and walks closer so she can stage-whisper in my ear, loud enough for Gus to hear.

"Do I need to save you from, like, whatever disaster is under there?" She points at his tray and about-to-burst backpack. "Should I bring you a change of clothes for when he spills again?"

"Actually, everything turned out really well," I tell her. "You'll see later!"

I'm surprised at how confident I sound and how much I believe it. Gus's face looks like someone just told him *Forbidden Treasure 4* is coming out tomorrow. Meanwhile, Darley's lips part in a sparkly, lip-glossed O.

"Wow," she says, "okay, well, go get 'em, champ."

Gus and I continue down the hall to the Cooking & Careers classroom. When I look back at Darley, she's winking and making kissy-faces at me. Is this some kind of message about her and Adrian? Have they kissed and she needs to play charades instead of telling me over text? (Gross.) But then I realize she's making kissy-faces and jutting her head at *Gus*. No. Surely she can't think that that's what *I* want to do. With *Gus Choi*, my former nemesis? No, no, no. Absolutely not. *Darley* is the boy-obsessed one. Not me. Nope, no, *nein*, *non*—

"Are you all right?"

"What?" I ask, but then I realize I've been shaking my head this whole time without knowing it. My throat starts to feel scratchy. I didn't say anything out loud, did I?

"Yeah," I squeak out, "I'm fine."

Gus shrugs. "Okey dokey." He gestures to the Cooking & Careers classroom door. "Race ya."

I rub my neck against my shirt collar in an effort to relieve some of the itchiness while my cooking partner once again gallops away from me without a care in the world, not at all concerned that his roast chicken might go flying. If he thinks I'm going to chase after him, he's bananas.

I take another careful step toward the classroom, clutching my appetizer and dessert. One thousand and one, one thousand and two, one thousand and three . . .

"Freya! I didn't know you were also a baker."

Mr. Keating is towering over me, examining my cookie through the cellophane like it's an artifact in a museum. I freeze, searching for Gus, who has already disappeared into the classroom and cannot save me from my orchestra conductor.

"I'm not," I mutter. "It's just for a project."

Mr. Keating strokes his chin. "Well, you've got lots of talents. Speaking of which, I wanted to talk to you about the competition."

Oh God, here it comes.

"Have you chosen your second piece yet?"

I want to say: *No, I have not picked out my second piece. I haven't even practiced in days. I don't know my music. I don't know anything.* To be honest, I forgot about the viola over the weekend, and it was kind of great, but now I immediately feel guilty because what would Dad say if he knew I thought that?

Instead I blurt, "Yeah. Uh, for the second piece, I'm thinking 'The Girl with the Flaxen Hair.'"

Again, it has a cool name, and Dad used to love to hear me play it.

My conductor's chin dips toward his chest. "'The Girl with the Flaxen Hair'?" he repeats. "That's not too much of a challenge, Freya. I think you could play something more difficult."

Does he think I have transformed into Paganini?

"I added some ornaments. And I think my attention to the dynamics will really help."

I truly have no idea what I'm talking about. Maybe I should add *world-class liar* to my list of so-called talents. It makes sense. Lying is a family trait.

Mr. Keating continues to stroke his chin. "Hmm. Can you drop by after last period? Say, two thirty? I'd like to hear it. We can figure this out." He glances down to where I'd usually be carrying my viola case. "You did, um, bring your instrument to school, right?"

"Yup." I nod, and at least this is true. "It's in the orchestra room. I'll come by after seventh."

He breathes a sigh of relief. "Perfect. See you later then."

"See you later."

And with that, my orchestra conductor prances away, leaving me with my cucumbers, my oversize chocolate chip cookie, and a whole lot of dishonesty. It's no big deal. I just have seven hours to relearn an entire song and convince Mr. Keating it's not an elementary piece so I don't have to learn something even harder for a county-wide orchestra competition in two weeks. And before that, present my dishes with Gus. As *real* bakers might say: piece of cake.

# CHOPSTICKS

"Are you ready?" Gus whispers.

I take a deep breath, feeling the air flow through me. "Ready as I'll ever be."

Sitting on the workbench before us are the uncovered foil tray with the steaming roast chicken just removed from reheating in the oven, the stir-fried ground beef and pickled cucumbers (best served chilled, Gus says), microwaved rice steaming in eleven china bowls, and a couple bottles of soy sauce. My chocolate chip cookie is in the warming drawer. Gus says that it's the surprise finale to our *fantastic meal*, but that kind of pressure makes my head spin.

Ms. Bethany prances around the classroom in a sunshine-yellow apron, doling out paper plates and plastic cutlery. We're second to go in the Cooking &

Careers lineup; on Monday, Nadine Bransford and Harrison Packer presented pizza rolls, chicken and vegetable paninis, and cupcakes for dessert. I have to say—our food *does* look way more professional, though that's really Gus's doing. Let's hope it *tastes* professional.

At our teacher's signal, Gus walks around to the front of the workbench and spreads his arms out wide. "I'm Gus Choi, and this is Freya June Sun."

"They already know who we are, Gus," I mumble.

But he just keeps rolling. "The theme for our menu today is French-Asian fusion with a legendary finale. First up, our appetizer is oyi namul, a Korean dish my mom taught me how to make. It's pickled cucumbers with ground beef and garlic. Hope none of you are vegetarians," he jokes.

"Well, I was *thinking* about it," Jonnell mutters.

*Crap.* We didn't even consider food preferences and allergies when making these dishes. The only stipulation Ms. Bethany gave us was to not use peanut butter. What if someone is allergic to soy sauce? Or hates chicken? Well, everyone liked the chicken paninis Nadine and Harrison made. What if they don't like *fancy* chicken?

Gus is clearly not thinking too hard about this because he gestures toward the oyi namul tray like a game-show host. I pick it up and dutifully carry it to each classmate's seat, making sure to spoon an equal portion onto everyone's plate. When I get to Darley's desk, she leans forward, pulling back her braids so they don't land in the food.

"Dude," she whispers, "this looks, like, *amazing*."

I feel myself grinning. Did Gus hear that? His harshest critic thinks his food looks *amazing*. Ms. Bethany takes an approving bite.

"De-lish-oussss," she slurs while chewing, and Gus looks positively thrilled.

While our classmates are devouring the appetizer, it's time to bring out the big guns: the herb-butter roast chicken and rice. I put a scoop of rice into each of the bowls, and Gus adds a few pieces of meat on top, which he then drizzles with warm butter sauce. I collect the paper plates while Gus passes out the bowls. I whip out chopsticks from a plastic shopping bag in my backpack. There are eleven pairs—just enough for Ms. Bethany and everyone in our class but us.

"For authenticity," I announce, "we have chopsticks for the entrée. But you can use your forks if you want—just for people who wanna try."

Surprisingly most of the students raise their hands, so I pass out the chopsticks. Last night, when I came up with the idea to bring chopsticks, Gus shouted, "Even *more* French-Asian fusion!" and then we rummaged through every drawer in his kitchen searching for leftover wooden chopsticks from old takeout orders. I think we kind of made a mess at the end—when I put on my sneakers to go home, I saw Allen slowly taking everything out of the drawers and putting it back in. Oops.

Gus and I watch and wait while the class digs in.

"Excellent!" Ms. Bethany proclaims, waving around her second bite of chicken smooshed between her chopsticks, "and what is this delicious *sauce*?"

"In addition to low-sodium soy sauce, we used pan juices from the roast chicken and combined them with melted butter and herbs for extra flavor," Gus explains.

In other words, Gus dumped all the chicken juice into a bowl, and I just threw in some chopped parsley like I was a flower girl tossing petals. It was pretty fun, even though I also got parsley all over the countertop. Double oops.

Gus lightly nudges my shoulder, and the brush of his arm against my elbow sends goose bumps up my sides. I try to rub them away.

"Almost go time," he whispers.

I nod, slowly walking back to the warming drawer to examine the deep-dish chocolate chip cookie inside. I hope everyone likes it. At least Ms. Bethany has "mmmed" and "de-lish-ousssed" to the appetizer and the main course, so we've nailed two out of the three so far. That's two thirds. Who even cares if people like my cookie then, right? I do the math in my head: Two thirds is approximately 67 percent. *Wait.* If this cookie bombs, we have a failing grade. Okay, I take it back. My enormous cookie determines if we pass or fail. Great.

I bend down and curl my fingers around the drawer handle like it's a roller-coaster lap bar and I'm bracing for a rapid, terrifying descent. Behind me, I hear Jonnell say that she's *stuffed* and Darley insist that there's always room for dessert, so I figure everyone is almost done eating. I clutch the handle even tighter. *Almost go time, Freya.* I whirl around for one final check on my classmates.

And that's when I see something disastrous. Not just disastrous—horrifying. Or as Dad would say:

Really,

really,

really

*bad luck.*

Of the ten kids in my Cooking & Careers class, six have their chopsticks jutting from the half-eaten rice, legs up, at ninety-degree angles in the china bowls. On a physical level, sure, it makes sense to stick your chopsticks in your rice bowls like that when you're done eating. But on any other level? It's *curse*-worthy.

Dad regaled me with the tale of the chopsticks over dim sum two autumns ago. We were visiting Grandma and Grandpa in Manhattan, so naturally, we made the trek to Chinatown to get dim sum. As I dug into the food, he told me that if I stuck my chopsticks in the rice, it would look like the incense sticks that we light at a funeral. And anything that reminds Chinese people of funerals? That equals extremely terrible luck.

My vision blurs, and all I can see is a roomful of pointy wood devil horns sprouting from the rice. When I blink, I notice Darley with her chopsticks nestled in the bowl, even though I've told her at least half a dozen times to never do that. We're doomed. *I'm* doomed.

It's all my fault. I should never have suggested we serve rice with Gus's roast chicken. I *definitely* should not have suggested chopsticks with the rice. I don't even know how to cook, much less bake, really. I bet everyone will think my cookie is disgusting. I should go back to what I know: orchestra and the viola. I should—

"And now, Freya will share her spectacular dessert with you!"

Gus is standing next to the workbench, his arms swept toward me as if I'm the final trick in a magic show. I feel the class's eyes boring into mine. But all *I* can see is their chopsticks.

"Um," I say, scooting back toward the exit, "excuse me."

"Freya?" Gus calls after me.

But I'm already halfway out the door.

# THE TRUTH

In the empty hallway, I practice the deep breathing I did earlier. *Inhale. Exhale.* But every time I breathe in, I see the ER doctor's face in the hospital when he told us what we were all dreading. *Exhale.* Back in the school hallway between rows of puke-green lockers. *Inhale.*

The kitchen with *The Canterbury Tales* still open-faced, like the world had just paused for a moment. Chopsticks in rice. My mother wailing. The screech of a bow against my viola's strings. May playing Taylor Swift at full blast. Dad's untouched shoes in the mudroom.

The classroom door swings open and shut. Sneakers tiptoe toward me.

"It's the chopsticks in the rice, right?"

I turn around. Gus is standing behind me, his hands wrapped around his rainbow-mime shirt.

"How did you know that?"

Gus shrugs. "It's a popular Korean superstition, too."

"It's not a *superstition*," I snap.

My armpits are wet with sweat, so I start fanning them, elbows flapping like chicken wings. Maybe Gus should have just served *me* as the main course. After running out of Cooking & Careers, I am as good as dead anyway.

"Okay," Gus relents, "not a superstition."

I stop flapping my arms, and he takes a step closer.

"Ms. Bethany wanted me to ask you . . . I mean I *also* wanted to ask you . . . Are you okay?"

*No.*

"Yes," I say.

My Cooking & Careers partner narrows his eyes. "*Errrr.* That was the lie detector test. It detects incorrect answers."

I shake my head. "That's not how lie detectors work."

"Well, that's how *mine* works."

"It's just . . ."

Should I really be telling Gus Choi my entire life story right after having an outburst in the middle of our cooking project?

Gus continues staring at me with those wide saucer eyes, a hesitant smile on his face. He doesn't look like he wants to run away or change the subject or laugh awkwardly like everyone else. So I tell him.

"It's just that"—I sniff—"my dad died last August, and he was really into signs, you know? Like red is good luck and white in your hair is bad and opening an umbrella indoors is, um, also bad and chopsticks in rice are . . ."

"Very bad," Gus finishes.

Searing heat floods my cheeks. "Yeah, very bad. So I just thought that if I could follow what he believed in, what he wanted . . . everything would be . . ." I struggle to find the words. "Everything would be . . . *okay*."

I let out a big sigh. I hope Gus doesn't think I'm ridiculous. I know May certainly does. And if Darley and Billie and other kids heard, they would laugh me out of the school. But Gus just crinkles his forehead.

"I get it. Or I get that I *don't* get it." He tilts his head to the side. "I'm sorry, Freya. That you're going through this. And that, like, your dad isn't here anymore. All this . . . It must feel overwhelming."

"Yeah," I whisper, "it does."

Somehow, saying that out loud makes me feel better, like the air in the hallway is lighter, looser. Part of me wants to grab Gus's hand, but I don't.

Gus scratches his mass of staticky hair. "Your deep-dish cookie is really great, Freya. And I think it would kinda suck if people couldn't eat it."

"No," I say flatly. "I can't go back in there."

What would they think? When the girl who fled

the classroom partway through her Cooking & Careers project returns? I can already picture Ms. Bethany's face shifting and contorting, the singsong, high-pitched quality to her voice when she says something like, *Ah good, Freya's back, let's continue!* I hate when she punctuates her sentences with exclamations, like they can wash away the awkwardness.

"Yeah, you can," Gus presses, "trust me. You wanna hear a secret? I'll let you in on my *biggest* secret yet."

I narrow my eyes. "What?"

"I know how to wipe people's memories."

"Uh-huh."

"I do!" Gus insists. "Want me to tell you how?"

I groan. "Fine. Tell me how."

"You give them a scrumptious deep-dish chocolate chip cookie. *Instant* memory wiper."

"Gus—"

"I'm serious! Do you know how many times I've used this technique when my parents have been mad at me? One second they promise they're gonna ground me for blah-blah-blah amount of days. But one bite of a fresh-from-the-oven cookie or even a well-made green bean . . ." He snaps his fingers. "Booyah. All is forgiven."

"That is a bald-faced lie, Gus Choi."

My Cooking & Careers partner steps even closer. "It

is the truth, Freya June Sun. I swear on all three editions of *Forbidden Treasure. Including* my expansion packs."

He holds up his hand like he's a Boy Scout even though he'd never make it through Boy Scouts because he's way too clumsy.

"And if that doesn't work," he adds, "I'll do something truly embarrassing so everyone will be thinking about that. After all, what's a Gus and Freya cooking presentation without a little entertainment?"

I giggle. Tears pearl on my lashes, and I can't tell if they're from laughter or sadness. Either way, at least Gus Weirdo Choi will be by my side.

"Okay," I say at last. "Let's go back in."

# PASSION

Everything happens the way I expect. Ms. Bethany's voice is sugar-sweet. Kids murmur in the back of the classroom. Darley won't look me in the eye.

But then Gus asks me to tell the class how I made the deep-dish cookie.

And I tell them. As he slices and serves, I talk about how putting in chocolate chips *and* chocolate chunks adds richness to the dough. (I learned that last night.) I talk about the gooey-to-crunch ratio. I even talk about what the cookie represents—at least to me. Sweatpants and fuzzy blankets. Weekend diner nights where the music in the background is *just* loud enough and everyone is laughing. Cozy evenings watching your favorite television show. Sleepovers with your best friends. At that, Darley looks up, chocolate smeared on the corners of her lips. She smiles, and I smile back.

Ms. Bethany clasps a paper plate between her hands. "Absolutely wonderful, Freya," she gushes, her voice finally a normal pitch. "This cookie could be served in a restaurant, that's how good it is. I particularly like the addition of the salt. And I love all the *feelings* it evokes. A-plus." She glances at Gus. "For the both of you."

Gus grins, and we fist-bump. We did it. We actually did it.

"Ka-pow," I whisper.

"Ka-pow, Freya," he whispers back.

For the rest of the day, I feel like I'm floating. Gus might be right about cookies being memory erasers because no one bothers me about my sudden disappearing act. At our lockers after school, Darley squeezes my arm and rambles to Adrian about how impressed she was with our food and how well Gus and I work together. When she says *that*, she winks, and I stick my tongue out at her.

Soon, she's rushing off to her soccer game, Adrian on her tail, while I twirl my locker dial and lean down to stuff my notebooks in my backpack. A throat clears behind me.

"Billie?" I say.

I haven't seen her all day. She usually joins us at our

lockers before first and last periods, but lately, she's been missing in action. She barely responds to Darley's texts anymore, occasionally answering homework questions with one-word answers. Then again, *I* barely respond to Darley's texts anymore.

I stay crouched and twist my shoulders to glance backward. But it's not Billie clearing her throat. It's Ms. Bethany.

"Oh," I say, standing up and simultaneously tripping over my feet. "Sorry, I thought you were somebody else."

Ms. Bethany smiles, pushing her slightly grown-out pixie behind her ears. Her hair is lilac this week, which is a new color for her. I will have to add it to her mood board.

"No worries, Freya," she says. "I just wanted to talk to you about something."

*Come on.* Do we really need to rehash the chopsticks-in-rice incident? Didn't we already get A-pluses?

"Sure," I say, crossing my arms.

I don't care how high-pitched my Cooking & Careers teacher's voice gets. I am not telling her about my dead dad's belief system.

"There's a school baking contest in about a week and a half. While a panel of students does vote for its favorite dishes, it's more about young bakers who love sharing their food with one another. If you want, you should participate. I've suggested the same thing to Gus, and he's already said yes."

Well, that's *not* how I thought this conversation was going to go.

"A baking contest?" I repeat. "But I'm not a baker."

Ms. Bethany tugs at her earrings—dangly beaded parrots with crimson feathers. They remind me of the pair of red birds. I peek out the skylight to see if their feet have landed on the ceiling, but they're nowhere to be found. No sign from Dad today.

"You baked a fantastic deep-dish cookie, Freya," she reminds me, "so you clearly have talent. But more importantly, you have *passion*."

"Passion?" I echo again.

*Passion* is for my sister, who breaks school rules because she cares so much about climate change and wants to be a journalist or an activist or a politician or maybe all three. No one has ever described *me* as passionate.

"Yes," Ms. Bethany confirms. "When you were talking about what chocolate chip cookies remind you of... Well, I thought that was just beautiful. Food *should* evoke memories and joy. And I could see how happy you were talking about what'd you created. I could see your passion."

My lips part, but I don't know what to say. Ms. Bethany makes sense, but at the same time, her words feel wrong.

My Cooking & Careers teacher pulls a peach flyer from her enamel pin–adorned satchel.

"The contest is May 4," she says. "Think about it."

"Okay," I tell her, "thanks."

As Ms. Bethany walks away, I unfold the paper and examine the bold block letters:

**HARTSWOOD ANNUAL STUDENT BAKING CONTEST**

**SATURDAY, MAY 4, FROM 10 A.M. TO 2 P.M.**

**TRUMAN GYMNASIUM IN THE UPPER SCHOOL**

Underneath are details about where to drop off your food and what awards are being handed out.

Saturday, May 4. Why does that date sound so familiar? May 4. May 4. Suddenly, I remember. The Westchester County Orchestra Competition is on May 4.

And then I remember something even more important. I'm late for my meeting with Mr. Keating.

# THE DISASTER CONTINUES

I'm panting by the time I rummage through my locker to find my old "The Girl with the Flaxen Hair" sheet music, race to the orchestra room to grab my viola, and sprint to Mr. Keating's office, my case banging against my thighs like I'm its personal punching bag.

When I knock on the door, I try really hard not to double over in pain. Mr. Keating twists the handle open, and I wipe away sweat for the second time today.

"Hi," I say, "I'm here."

Mr. Keating frowns, turning his wrist so I can see his watch. The time reads 2:45.

"You're late, Freya." He doesn't even sound angry, just disappointed.

My heart plummets into my toes. The hardness in his voice could be my dad's.

"Sorry," I say, "I just got . . . Well, a teacher wanted . . ."

Mr. Keating waves his hand back and forth before pulling up a chair, the legs squealing against the tile.

"It's fine." He sighs. "Just tune your viola and we'll get started."

I try to revive my sinking heart as I slump in the plastic chair and tune my viola to an A on the keyboard. I didn't get a chance to practice today like I thought I would. Or more like I *forgot*—I could have skipped lunch to practice, but I was too busy eating Gus's KitKats. In study hall, I went to the library and absentmindedly looked at dessert recipes on my phone between studying for my social studies test tomorrow and eavesdropping on the lacrosse girls' gossip. When did I get like this? The Freya from a few months ago or even a few weeks ago would have dashed to the computer room to reprint her music, make new notes, and ensure that "The Girl with the Flaxen Hair" was played perfectly by the end of the day. The Freya from a few weeks ago would have never been late to a meeting with her orchestra conductor.

I gulp, familiarizing myself with the eighth notes, the pianos, the fortes, the crescendos. Here goes nothing.

When I play, I am on autopilot, remembering the way Dad used to sway with the sweeping, repeating melody. The Debussy piece was originally written for piano, but Dad always thought it was richer on the viola, like dark-chocolate gelato—sweet in its bitterness. I stumble through the last run and wince, hoping Mr. Keating doesn't notice, though I know he does. The piece finally ends, and I force a vibrato to make it sound more impressive than it actually is.

Mr. Keating clears his throat. "Well," he says, "that was pretty."

The way he says *pretty* does not make it sound like it's a good thing.

"Pretty, but just not challenging enough for your level, Freya," he clarifies.

Ah, going straight for the jugular. I nod, speechless.

"And even then . . . you didn't play with a lot of *heart*," he continues. "It felt almost robotic at times? I'm surprised, Freya, considering how well you know this piece."

I swallow hard. *How well you know this piece . . .* The last time I played "The Girl with the Flaxen Hair" was for Dad. And now I've pretty much forgotten it. Now I am *robotic*.

My sheet music swirls before me. I try to picture Dad like I am taking a photo of him. His unruly black hair, long, gangly frame, reading glasses, mischievous smile. But what about his voice when he hummed along to my viola playing? What about that special laugh he had when he was particularly pleased with my performance?

I'm trying to remember them clearly, but I can't. I'm forgetting. I'm *forgetting* Dad.

"Freya?" Mr. Keating's tone has changed from brittle to soft. "Is everything A-okay with you?"

"Uh-huh," I say immediately. "I'm fine."

My orchestra conductor picks at his fingernails and then drums them against the keyboard.

"It's—it's been a difficult year for you," he stammers, "and if there's anything you want to discuss with me... Well, I, um, I am sure I can be of *some* use..."

"Thanks, Mr. Keating," I say to save us both from misery, "but don't worry about it."

I restack my sheet music and quickly shove it back into my backpack. The last thing I want to talk about with my orchestra conductor is Dad. Or the viola. Or any of this.

"I'll pick a better piece," I tell him, "and I'll practice this week. What about... Biber's Passacaglia in G Minor?"

I hate the Passacaglia. It's hard and super long, there are a ton of skips, and it is somehow at the same time extremely boring to play.

Mr. Keating sits up. "Passacaglia is perfect!"

Of course it is. I smile with all my teeth. "Awesome. I'll start working on that tonight."

I loop my backpack straps over my shoulders and leave before he can suggest I play something even harder.

Once I'm out of his office and in the orchestra wing, I try to picture Dad again. Puffy hair just like mine. Gangly frame. That giddy laugh when he thought I'd played perfectly. Thank goodness, I remember now.

The red birds have sent me many signs to enter this competition and play for him, and I've been messing it all up by being unfocused. I can't forget anything about Dad. Especially what he wanted for me.

# INSPIRATION

I practice the Passacaglia and Mr. Keating's other competition piece for me, Bohm's Sarabande, that night just like I said I would. And the night after that. And the night after that. And the night after *that*. I ignore Darley's still-constant texts about Adrian. I bail out of Billie's sleepover (not that she's reminded us about it anyway). I respond to Gus's memes with emojis. I pretend not to hear Mom and May arguing upstairs about who knows what, their stomping so loud and raised voices so constant, they create an off-kilter rhythm.

Passacaglia. Stomp, stomp. More Passacaglia. Stomp, yell, *yell*, and the grand finale: door slam.

By the time Wednesday evening rolls around, my hands are stiff and cramped, and there are permanent string indents on my finger pads. Mom pokes her head into the living room to tell me she's going to bed early, which is her nice way of asking me to stop playing the viola. It's 9 p.m., and I don't know what to do. I am too wired to go to sleep. I don't want to study for my science quiz. I certainly don't want to see what May's up to, since I can hear her whispering on her cell in her bedroom. At least if she sneaks out again, I'll catch her, since the staircase is across from the living room.

I stare out the window. The black night sky fills every corner of the glass frame, crickets chirping through the silence. My phone pings. Gus has sent his idea for the Hartswood baking contest—he's using his parents' Instant Pot to make yaksik, which he tells me is sweetened rice with dried fruits and nuts. I don't like dried fruit, but he promises me I'll like yaksik. Gus is very confident about his cooking, even when it's technically baking, which he says is *not* his specialty.

*It's yours*, he writes with a winky face followed by a super happy face.

I'm too tired to analyze his winky face. Besides, baking is *not* my specialty. It's just calming, like spending the day at a beach is to my mother and sneaking out on a school night apparently is to my sister. I pull the latches shut on my viola case and traipse into the empty kitchen. On the counter is my take-home folder, and underneath is Ms. Bethany's peach baking contest flyer, which I have memorized at this point. I keep thinking back to my deep-dish cookie, the way the chocolate oozed when I broke it apart, the way the crack of the egg and the whir of the mixer felt like my personal symphony.

Even if I don't enter the contest, I can still have my symphony, at least just for the night. I open the fridge and peek inside. There's surprisingly more than normal in there, which is probably because Grandma and Grandpa went to the grocery store when they visited. Butter and eggs and, of course, lots of fruit. I look around the kitchen some more. The cabinets are brimming with barely used bags of walnuts and almonds because Grandpa always says he's going to eat them and then forgets. On the top shelf is a sack of flour, which Grandma bought so we could make dumplings as a family, though we never do because Mom is never home long enough to make them. Behind it is an old box of sugar. (Does sugar go bad? Who knows.)

I lay out all the potential ingredients on the kitchen table like I'm back in the Cooking & Careers classroom and Ms. Bethany is encouraging us to *get creative.*

There's no creativity in orchestra, though Mr. Keating always thinks that there is. There are methods. Dad had a foolproof one for learning orchestra pieces.

Step 1: Listen to recordings (but not amateur ones—professional ones).

Step 2: Examine the score.

Step 3: Break the music into sections.

I survey the ingredients spread out on the table once more and separate the refrigerated stuff like butter and eggs from the dry stuff like flour and nuts. Do these count as sections?

I keep squinting at everything, but no amazing recipe comes to mind. It's not as simple as learning a new orchestra piece. When I was little, I could learn an entire song in a week or less. Once, at age six, I used Dad's step-by-step method to memorize "Ode to Joy" in two hours. I played it at Mom's book club that she used to run and watched my parents pretend to be humble as all the aunties cooed over my "natural talent" and adorable, chubby fingers. Afterward, Dad was so thrilled, he snuck me out to the Chinese bakery even though he'd knew it would ruin my dinner and Mom would be mad. It did ruin my dinner, and she *was* mad. Still, it was worth it. We stuffed our faces with egg tarts, lotus seed buns, pineapple cakes, and hup toh soh. I miss that bakery. I haven't been in years.

I look back at the ingredients. They seem different than they did minutes ago. *Get creative.* Walnuts. Flour. Sugar. Eggs. Baking powder. Baking soda. Butter. Salt. I find a recipe online, quickly skim it, and then click off my phone screen. *I can do this.*

I preheat the oven and drop to the bottom cabinet and pull out a glass mixing bowl to literally get cracking. I try to be as quiet as possible, so May and Mom don't come downstairs and ask questions I don't want to answer.

I know exactly what to make.

# MOVIE NIGHT

"I can't *believe* she brought Adrian," Billie mutters.

It's Friday night and the premiere of *The Everlasting Sisters*, which is a movie about three immortal sisters who go to battle against an evil totalitarian government. Billie, Darley, and I have been wanting to see this for ages, especially since we read and loved the book series. I'd forgotten the premiere was tonight until Billie texted this morning with a calendar invite. Even though I should be practicing the Passacaglia until my fingers bleed since the competition is tomorrow, I still said *yes* to the movie. This is first time Billie has texted the group chat in ages. Though now that we're actually at the theater, her frown is so wide, it could take up the entire *Everlasting Sisters* life-size poster we're standing next to.

I shift from sneaker to sneaker on the maroon, zigzag

carpet. Darley and Adrian are standing in front of us in the refreshments line, *just* far enough that they can't hear Billie's not-so-quiet grumbling.

"I don't even know how she got him a ticket," Billie whines. "It was sold out when I checked this afternoon. *Sold out.*"

I shrug. "Maybe he already had a ticket?"

Billie snorts. "And was going by himself? Yeah right."

We step forward, and Billie shoots invisible laser beams at Darley's and Adrian's intertwined hands. I should care more that Darley surprise-invited Adrian to our movie night without asking first. But as Billie glowers with anger, all I can think about is a *different* kind of heat: the oven where I took out my crackly, buttery hup toh soh. I made the Chinese walnut cookies Wednesday and perfected them last night. They were melt-on-your-tongue delicious. I swear they tasted just like the ones at the bakery.

I placed them in a plastic container and slid them into my backpack before Mom and May woke up in the morning. I'm not sure if I'm going to submit them to the baking contest yet, especially because I don't know if I'll have time to put them in the gymnasium after I perform for the judges at the orchestra competition.

Billie stops complaining long enough to tap my shoulder. "Can we get popcorn together?" Her voice is timid and small, like I might say no.

"Yeah, of course," I say. I buy us the biggest one, and she finally breaks into a real smile.

*The Everlasting Sisters* is jam-packed, like Billie said it would be. We squeeze past another canoodling couple (Billie side-eyes them as if they, too, have personally wronged her) and plop down in our seats. I'm the physical barricade between Darley and Billie, though Darley doesn't know it. I turn to her and pretend I don't see Adrian's hairy arm smooshed against her back.

"This is gonna be great," I say with enough energy to power a school bus.

Darley nods. "I know, I'm sooooo excited."

I whip my head toward Billie and telepathically say: *See? She's sooooo excited.* Billie is not convinced.

And you know, maybe she's right because when the commercials are over and the lights dim, Darley is not even looking at the three sisters standing imposingly in the desert. She's looking at Adrian.

"See, I told you," Billie hisses.

I just pat her shoulder so she'll stop talking during the movie. These are my two hours of freedom. If I focus hard enough, I can wipe everything away: my annoying friends, the viola, tomorrow's *two* competitions that simultaneously makes me want to squeal and throw up. It's just me and Tatiana, Adella, and Valentine. Three girls who, unlike me, know exactly what they want. They move from mysterious desert to ravaged countryside to the chancellor's steel, black mansion. They are begging him to release their parents, who are imprisoned for protesting the government's cruel policies. The chancellor drags the handcuffed mother and father out to the ballroom to torture the sisters. I rub the back of my neck. I don't remember this happening in the books.

Then, as the father taunts the chancellor and the girls tell him to stop, the chancellor kills him. You don't see it happen, just a sword, blood on the gray ceramic, and the thud of a body. The audience gasps. My mind is whirring.

I *swear* this didn't happen in the books. Why is the screenwriter doing this? Why is this happening? The sisters are screaming now. Adella is on her knees, reaching for her dead father. And all I can think is: *Dad waving goodbye to me the morning he left for the office, how I didn't know it would be his last. How oblivious I was. How I wasn't there, how he's not here, how I couldn't do anything then, and how I can't do anything now.*

*Stop, Freya, stop.* But the movie's music pulses louder and louder in my ears. My heart is thumping. This didn't happen in the books. This *didn't* happen in the books.

I try to root myself in the theater, but Darley is nuzzling Adrian and giggling, clearly not paying attention to the film. On my left, Billie is texting, her phone squished between her legs. When I glance down to see what on earth she could be writing, I realize she's texting *me* about *Darley*. Like somehow whipping out her phone and typing messages is better than complaining in my ear.

*The accounting office. Dad's loafers on the carpet.* I am breathing really quickly now. I try to calm down, but I'm not sure I can. Billie's phone goes dark.

"Freya?" she whispers. "What's wrong?"

I don't want to talk to her. I just want to get out of here.

"Freya?"

I stand up and climb over Billie's knees and the canoodling couple's feet. They grumble at me for blocking their view, but I ignore them. In the aisle, I wonder if everyone is staring at me. I hear Darley's voice: "Ow, Billie! Stop poking!"

Billie's shrieks cut right through the theater. "You were too busy cuddling with this *random boy* to notice your *friend's* in the aisle having some kind of an *anxiety attack*!"

Yup, everyone's *definitely* staring at me. I don't stop to hear what Darley says back. Instead, I dive into the nearest bathroom and lock myself in the corner stall. I text my mom to come pick me up early and ignore her when she asks why. *Just come*, I write, and thankfully, she does.

# THE COMPETITION

When I don't answer any of Mom's questions in the car, she sighs and gives up, letting me lean my head against the window and pretend to fall asleep. At home, I crawl into bed and scroll through twenty texts from Billie and Darley before shutting off my phone. We have Monday off for a teacher workshop day, so I won't have to see them for a whole eighty-four hours. I hope they're happy being annoying to each other.

In the morning, a bad, squeaky pop song blares through my alarm clock's speakers, and the smells of greasy bacon and cinnamon toast waft through the crack under my door. Mom's gone all out for breakfast, which means she's either *super* excited about the orchestra competition or she feels bad about yesterday. Either way, I want to disappear.

Since I can't, I pull out a pale-pink daisy dress from my closet and pair it with a tan crochet sweater with a satin front tie. I look like an eighty-five-year-old grandma, but it will have to do.

Downstairs, Mom and May are at the kitchen table, a plate of toast and bacon perched before my empty chair.

"Good morning," Mom says in a too-chipper voice that sounds like she's talking to one of her economics students. "Did you sleep well?"

"Fine," I mumble. I hold up a piece of bacon. "Thanks for making breakfast."

"I haven't done it in a while," she admits, "but I thought you could use some protein before your big competition. I hope I didn't burn the bacon."

She did, but I don't tell her. My mother fiddles with a button on her blouse as I chew.

"Your sister is going to take my car and drive you to the upper school this morning, by the way. I have to finish up some work for the conference."

Oh right, Mom has some economics convention in Manhattan tomorrow. May's supposed to stay home and babysit me, which means she'll go out with her friends and leave me to fend for myself.

"Okay," I say.

Mom dabs at her lips with a napkin. "Guess we both have big weekends ahead of us. Right, Freya?"

"Uh-huh."

May, meanwhile, is not contributing to this conversation at all. She cowers over her phone as she bites into a piece of toast, her knees tucked under her stretched-out tie-dye sweatshirt. When Mom nudges her, she wipes some loose crumbs from her mouth and slams her phone on the table.

"We're leaving in ten," May declares.

Have I mentioned that my sister is the worst? I dump half my breakfast in the trash and bring my dishes to the sink. As I watch the water slide down the plate, I think about the hup toh soh sitting in my backpack in the living room. My performance slot is at nine, and the baking contest doesn't start until ten, so I don't know if I'll be able to submit the cookies before May gets tired of waiting around and drives home without me. (She literally would, too.) Despite everything, I still want to try to hand them off to Ms. Bethany. It's not that I care about winning an award. I just want someone to taste my walnut cookies and enjoy them. I stick my plate in the dishwasher. I have to get someone to enjoy my music instead.

While May laces up her combat boots, I grab my backpack and viola case. Mom follows us into the mudroom, her slippers tapping against the tile. She smooths out my hair and pats my cheek like she did on the staircase the night I got home from Gus's.

"You're going to do great, Freya," she says. "Your dad would be so proud of you."

That entire sentence makes me want to disintegrate. May doesn't say anything half as nice. In fact, she doesn't say much at all. On the drive to the upper school, she turns up the music streaming from her Spotify playlist and flares her nostrils like she's upset with the road.

We pull into the parking lot, dotted with scattered cars with parents probably inside, drumming their fingers nervously against their steering wheels as they wait for their children to perform some mediocre sonatas. The upper school's brick facade casts a shadow over the pavement like an ominous dark cloud. May clicks off the music.

"Good luck," she says dully, "I'll be here."

I give her a half-hearted thumbs-up that she doesn't see because she's back to being hunched over her phone. I step out of the car and slide on my backpack straps, careful not to jostle the cookies inside. Then I grab my viola from the back seat and head inside.

No red birds serenade my entrance.

In the lobby, there are two signs attached to black metal posts. The first says, HARTSWOOD BAKING CONTEST THROUGH HERE! The second says, WESTCHESTER COUNTY ORCHESTRA COMPETITION with an arrow pointing to the left. Straight ahead, the cafeteria's double doors are propped open, and I glimpse rows of tables covered with white plastic tablecloths. Above them hangs a colorful triangular banner. Angular letters spell out BAKING CONTEST. There doesn't seem to be anyone in the room yet—no judge or monitor to register with. I turn left like I'm supposed to.

The upper school hallways have been transformed into waiting areas with folding chairs lined up against the walls. A woman at a desk in the front of the hall looks up at me and beams. Her nametag says, SASHA GU, VOLUNTEER.

"Hello! Signing in?"

I nod, and she slides over a sheet of paper. "Find your name on the list and write your signature next to it."

I line my finger up with the trail of last names until I see *Sun, Freya June. Viola. 9:00 a.m.* It makes me official. The *last* thing I want to be is official. I finish writing my name and scoot past Sasha Gu, Volunteer. The hem of my floral grandma dress tickles my knees as I try to find an empty folding chair. There are kids everywhere with trumpets and French horns and violins and cellos. I spot Xena running through her scales under a skylight. She's wearing a bright-red dress with deep-red lipstick, her hair gelled into a sleek bun. I duck behind a trombone so she doesn't see me. I'm glad she's here and hope she does well, but I do *not* want another person witnessing me choke this weekend. Then I realize the person with the trombone is Auntie Tsu's son, Garrett, because of course it is. Thankfully, he doesn't recognize me. Guess our lack of churchgoing is really paying off these days.

I finally find a seat by a gaggle of flutists and take out my Passacaglia music. Dotted eighth notes swirl on the page. I've played this song at least forty times this weekend, and yet the thought of playing it one more time makes a ball the size of a ten-pound avocado grow in the pit of my stomach. I close my music and open it again, but still my stomach churns, and the avocado balloons. What if I *actually* throw up?

Blue morning sky peeks through the skylight above Xena's head. I stare at the glass and start begging.

*Tell me not to play, Dad. Send me a sign.*

I'll take anything. Mysterious birds. A spilled milkshake. A flash of lightning. A building collapsing, perhaps?

Instead, Sasha Gu, Volunteer, clears her throat.

"Freya June Sun? It's your turn to play."

# THE SIGN

Walking into the room is like walking into a movie in slow motion. I see my feet move across the floor. I see the viola and bow shaking in my palms. The judges say their names (which I barely hear) and push up their glasses and write notes down on big pieces of paper. Someone says something about Mr. Keating and how I am his star pupil, and I have no idea what I'm doing on the outside, but on the inside, bile is gurgling in the back of my throat.

I tell them that I didn't get a chance to tune in the hall, and they say that's not a problem, and someone plays a note on the piano (There's a pianist? When did he get here? When did this piano show up?), and I tune accurately or poorly—I'm not sure.

I set my sheet music on the stand. A judge says, "Let's start with the Passacaglia," and I nod or laugh or whimper or a combination of the three. *You can do this, Freya*, a voice in my head rallies. When I don't start playing, it turns mean and insistent. *You* have *to do this, Freya. For Dad.*

That's when I see them. Through the window behind Judge 1's head. Two red birds with rigid, closed wings and pinched, judgmental beaks. Those freaking birds. It's the surest sign I know. The clearest message from Dad that I need to play. But I can't.

I can't.

I can't.

*I can't.*

"I'm so sorry, Dad," I whisper.

Judge 2 looks up from her paper. "Ms. Sun? We're ready when you are."

"I'm sorry," I say, louder this time so that all the judges tilt their chins and wrinkle their noses and open their mouths to speak.

But before they can protest, I grab my sheet music, backpack, and viola case.

"I'm sorry," I say again as I dash out of the room.

# PANIC

The hallway seems larger as I sprint through it—a blur of formal dresses and blazers and shiny-gold instruments. I don't think about anything but the red birds as I weave through the crowd. How I let them down. How I let *Dad* down. I enter the lobby, the mass shifting from instrumentalists to bakers with towers of treats. They stroll into the cafeteria jabbering about cake and icing like those are their only concerns. I wish I could be like that. But I'm not.

I have to get out of here. I turn sharply toward the lobby doors. As I'm speed-walking, a plastic container whams right into my side.

"Oh my gosh, I'm sorry!"

I look up. It's Gus Choi and his yaksik.

"Freya!" he says. He's touching my side, his soft hand wrapped around my rib cage. "Are you okay?"

Mm-hmm. Yep. Perfect.

"Not really," I blurt. "Is your yaksik all right? I hope I didn't ruin it."

"Don't worry. It's fine."

Gus's voice is soothing and gentle, his forehead creased because he's permanently worried about Freya June Sun, the walking disaster. He releases his hand from my side, and I chew on my lip, pulling my viola case to my chest.

"Hey," he says gently, "at least nothing spilled this time, right? No flying milkshakes?"

I half smile.

"Or exploding avocados."

"Or exploding avocados." He laughs. "So it's a win." He jerks his head to the cafeteria. "Are you coming in? We can register together."

I shake my head. I really do have to get out of here. Just a hundred feet away are three judges probably calling Mr. Keating up to tell him that his *star pupil* is a complete black hole of disappointment. I imagine their steely voices, Mr. Keating's flustered response as he tries to excuse what I did.

"Why not?" Gus asks. "Did your audition go okay?"

I'm not listening to him. Instead, the red birds zoom back at full speed in my mind, their horrible red wings and horrible beaks and horrible beady eyes. They must hate me. Dad must hate me.

Wet, salty liquid hits the corner of my mouth, and I realize I'm crying. Streaming tears are dripping down my chin. I avoid Gus's face and whip out the hup toh soh from my backpack.

"I gotta go," I say, shoving the cookies in his hands, "but take these."

Gus wobbles with the treat stack now covering half his face. "To bring in for the baking contest?"

I shake my head. "No. I just can't look at them anymore."

I can't have them weighing down my backpack like an albatross. An albatross that made me mess up my competition and shock the judges and ignore the red birds and let Dad down. I wave chaotically at the doors.

"Just give them to your parents or something. They're hup toh soh. Chinese walnut cookies. Maybe they'll like them. Or you can throw them out. I really don't care."

"Freya, are you—"

"Bye, Gus."

And for the second time today, I'm running away.

# MAY'S ADVICE

The parking lot is overflowing now, cars squished together like it's a school day and not a random spring weekend. May is still in the same position as before, knees up in the driver's seat, her face bent over her phone. I try to wipe away my tears with the back of my sweater sleeve, but when she looks up, she notices my puffy eyes and flushed face as I crawl into the car.

"What's wrong with you?" she asks. "Did the prodigy not perform well?"

"I'm not a prodigy," I snap. "I never said I was, and I hate that people call me that."

My sister's eyes widen in surprise. She clicks her phone off and drops it in the cupholder.

"Okay," she says slowly, "sorry. Got it."

I wipe snot from my nose as May examines my rumpled dress and smudged lip gloss.

"What happened?"

Her voice sounds different, like she actually cares for once, but I don't know how to begin. I pinch the wrinkles in my dress.

"Let's just go," I say.

But May isn't moving her legs or turning on the engine. She swivels around to see my viola case strewn across the back seat.

"You know, Freya," she begins as if we're playing a game of hangman and she's trying to choose every letter carefully, "if you don't want to play the viola or whatever, you don't have to."

My jaw instantly clenches. "Yes, I do."

"But, like, seriously, you don't." She shrugs. "No one will be upset if you quit."

I twist my neck to look her in the eye. "What do you mean? Of course people will be upset."

"Okay, who?"

"My conductor."

"Who gives a crap what he thinks?"

"Mom."

"She'll get over it."

I feel my shoulders tense. Why do I suddenly want to scream?

"And Dad," I say, choking out the words. "Dad will be really, really upset."

May tosses a hand in the air like all I've told her is that I don't like pineapples on pizza.

"Dad's not here." She sniffs.

*Dad's not here?* That's what she has to say in response? *Our* dad, the one we lived with and loved our entire lives? The one who basically memorized all my music, who took me to all my rehearsals and concerts and stood up for the freaking Hallelujah Chorus? The one who sent two red birds just to remind me that I needed to keep going and I ignored him and gave up?

"He's still here," I tell her, "even though he's gone."

"I don't know what you're talking about."

Of course she doesn't. She doesn't see what I see.

"You know how Dad said pairs are lucky? And the color red?"

May's face is blank. I continue.

"Well, Dad has sent a pair of red birds every time I felt like I didn't want to play the viola to remind me that I *need* to. Yeah, you heard that right—*red birds*. And there are no regular red birds other than cardinals in Westchester, so they're definitely magical or spiritual or something, and they're definitely *real*. And he sent them today, *during* my audition, so I knew that was a sign to play, and I didn't play because I couldn't for some reason, and now I've disappointed him *and* the magical birds."

The words finish tumbling out of me. I'm crying again, and I wipe more tears away with the backs of my now-snot-covered sleeves. My sister is silent. Maybe she's finally listening, finally understanding.

"Freya," she says.

I sit forward, ready for May to admit that she's been wrong this entire time.

"Dad's superstitions are just that. *Superstitions.* They're silly and ridiculous and for children. You're thirteen now. You need to grow up."

I freeze in my seat, speechless. The words spin like a Ferris wheel: *Silly. Ridiculous. For children. You need to grow up.* My sister turns to the windshield and starts the ignition. I'm not crying anymore when the next words come flying out of my mouth.

"You suck," I spit. "You suck, and you never cared about Dad at all. Not the way I do. He clearly means *nothing* to you."

May's hands are still on the steering wheel. She doesn't look in my direction. I jerk my seat belt over my body, and we both flinch when it snaps into place. Finally, she speaks.

"I'm driving you home," she says calmly, "and then I never want you to speak to me ever again."

# UNRAVELING

When we pull into the garage, Mom waves from the mudroom and ushers May and me inside. She's asking a lot of questions that we answer with one-word responses.

*How was the competition?*

*Fine.*

*Did the judges like your pieces?*

*Yes.*

*Was there a lot of traffic on the way back?*

*No.* (This one is true, at least.)

In the kitchen, a spread of roast beef and pastrami sandwiches with pickles and potato salad lines the counter. Mom must have stopped by the deli in town for this little surprise celebration after the competition. Great.

"I need to go upstairs," I announce.

"Mmm?" Mom says.

She's standing over the water pitcher, so she's not really listening. I scoot past her and almost bump into May, who is pulling out a chair to sit down at the table. True to her word, she acts like I'm invisible. My sister gnaws on a pickle at maximum volume. I clomp out of the kitchen and up to my room as she continues to chew like she's trying to crunch out the sound of my footsteps.

I swing open my bedroom door and throw my unzippered backpack on the carpet. Sheet music spills out, but I don't bother to pick it up. Instead, I fling myself onto the bed and pull the comforter over my head. I hear the moment Mom realizes that something's wrong. I listen as she puts the puzzle pieces together one by one. *What happened?* she's asking May. *What's wrong with you girls? I thought Freya said the competition went well. Did you say something to her?*

Eventually, my sister starts spilling her guts, and Mom's voice gets louder and May's voice gets louder, and their muffled yelling reverberates through my walls. I stuff the blanket into my ears. I don't want to hear what they're saying anymore.

They argue for minutes or maybe hours. When I peek out from under the comforter, I spot slivers of golden sky between my window's blinds. I wonder if Gus is home yet. I wonder if the birds have found me again and are waiting on a tree branch in my front yard. No, they probably despise me. They probably won't return.

May's words poison my tongue: *superstitions*, *silly*, *ridiculous*, *grow up*. I think about what I shot back, the way May's face shifted into something like hurt. I roll over to the other side of the mattress. I don't care. If May doesn't want to talk to me for the rest of her life, so be it. I don't need a terrible, mean sister.

My stomach growls, and I ignore it. There's no way I'm going back downstairs. The heat from my comforter and the exhaustion from crying make me sleepy, and soon, I start to drift off.

I wake up to the sound of our doorbell ringing every five seconds. Then I hear a patter of slippers, a yank of a door handle, and Mom's cheery, fake post-fight voice: *Oh, hello! What can I do for you?* I can't hear what the mystery person is saying in response. Their conversation only lasts a few seconds, though, because soon the door clangs shut and the slippers patter back to the kitchen. Wait, no. I hear them on the staircase. In the hall. By my door. *Super.* Now Professor Julie Sun needs to yell at her second daughter.

My mother swings open my bedroom door without knocking. She looms over me, one hand on her hip, the other holding a roast beef sandwich on a white-glass plate.

I can already imagine the lecture I'm about to receive: *How could you leave the audition? How could you embarrass your family like this? You will have to make it up somehow. You will have to prove yourself even harder in Mr. Keating's select orchestra. You will have to—*

"You must be hungry," Mom says, stretching out her arm so that the plate hovers over my bedspread.

I take the food. I don't want to eat while her hand is still on her hip, her slippers digging into my fuzzy faux-shearling carpet, but my stomach grumbles again, and the smell of roast beef is too tantalizing. I bite into the sandwich and immediately close my eyes. I'd forgotten how much I love this deli.

My mother relaxes her power pose and perches on the corner of my bed.

"So," she says slowly, "sounds like you had quite the morning."

*Here we go.*

"You left the competition early."

"Uh-huh."

"And then you ran into the car, crying."

"Uh-huh."

"And then you and your sister got in a fight."

I place the plate on the nightstand and fold the pillow over my head so that *I* am the meat in its sandwich.

"Uh-huh," I say again, my voice muffled.

Mom sighs, and I brace myself for her lecture. But instead, she gently pulls my hands from the pillow and looks at me with this strange, open expression.

"You know, Freya," she says, fiddling with her wedding ring, "when I picked you up from the movie theater early last night and you didn't want to answer any of my questions, I thought it was best to give you space. But I'm not sure that was the right call." She pauses. "I think you have a lot going on in your head right now, and I want you to tell me. I want you to feel *comfortable* telling me."

She brushes a fleck of mascara off my cheek, and I notice her hand is shaking. It's weird seeing my mother as nervous as I am.

"I'm a single mom now, Freya. And I've been really focused on making sure that you and May have the same life as you did before."

"That's why Grandma and Grandpa are helping to pay for stuff," I blurt.

Mom grimaces. "I guess nothing gets past you girls, does it?" She fiddles with the tufts on my comforter. "I should have *never* listened to those church ladies and put us all in therapy immediately."

"What?"

"Never mind," Mom says, "we'll talk about that later. Anyway, yes, I've been so focused on bills and work that I haven't had a chance to check in with you emotionally.

And you've always been my quiet one, Freya. You've always kept everything in." She runs her fingers through my frizzy hair. "But I'm listening now. I promise."

I try to hold back tears, but they waterfall down my cheeks. Why am I always crying? Mom sits there patiently like nothing in the universe exists but us two. I breathe in boogers and tears and the smell of roast beef and Mom's floral perfume. *I want you to tell me. I'm listening.*

I stare at my sheet music, strewn across my floor.

"I don't want to play the viola anymore," I say.

I wait for a moment, but the plate on the nightstand doesn't shatter into a thousand pieces, my mother doesn't scream, and the ceiling doesn't come crashing in on us. I keep going.

"I don't want to play the viola, but Dad loved that I played the viola—I mean, he was so proud of me, and he thought I was gonna be a professional violist, and if I stop playing, he'll be really mad. I'll be disappointing him, even in heaven. And . . . and . . ." I point at the sheet music on the floor. "This is all that I have left of him."

It feels ridiculous to say, but it's true. The music *is* my dad. And ditching it feels like I'm ditching him. Mom pulls my body toward her and yanks me into a hug so tight, I can feel her heartbeat pounding against mine.

"Freya," she whispers against my neck, "you can never disappoint your dad. Because all he wanted was for you and May to be happy. I promise if Dad were here right now and you told him you really didn't like the viola and wanted to quit, he would be just fine. He loves you so much. And he is proud of you *no matter what.*"

"Really?" I say, my voice small.

"Really. Even if you don't play the viola."

She kisses my forehead. "You're going to grow up, Freya, and do things that your dad won't be able to weigh in on. But he's always going to be a part of you, okay? He's not going anywhere."

I nod. "Okay." I'm not sure I believe her yet, but I want to.

My mother wipes away tears and pulls out something from her back pocket. It's a bronze medal with a large number three ringed by stars hanging from a blue ribbon.

"Your friend Gus dropped this off. It turns out you won third place at your school's baking contest."

"What? I did?"

I can't believe it. People *ate* my hup toh soh? And they *liked* them?

"Wait a second," I say, "I didn't even enter. I told Gus to throw my cookies away."

"Well," Mom says with a smile, "I'm glad he didn't. I guess your friend knows you better than you thought."

She's right. He really *does.* I close my eyes and imagine the jury of my schoolmates biting into buttery, crumbly walnut cookies and enjoying them enough to vote for me. Something like pride blooms inside my chest. Or maybe it's joy.

"I didn't know you liked to bake," Mom says.

I scratch the top of my head. "It's a recent development," I admit. "It makes me feel calm, and it's kinda fun."

Mom smiles. "Well, then, it sounds wonderful."

# FAMILY TIME

That night, I don't dream. In the morning, I open my eyes and squint at the pale-yellow light drenching my bedroom walls. I tuck my comforter under my chin. Mom's words ring in my ears.

"He is proud of me no matter what," I whisper aloud. "Even if I don't play the viola."

The words feel foreign in my mouth, like I'm speaking a language I don't know. How can Mom be sure Dad's not mad? What about the red birds and the umbrella and the chopsticks?

I rip off the comforter and swivel my body on the bed so my feet are touching the floor. My sheet music is still sprawled out on the carpet. Crouching down, I pick up the papers and tidy them into a stack. I could put them downstairs with my viola case where they belong. I could toss them into the trash can. Instead, I shove the music in a wicker basket beneath my desk.

Downstairs, I find Mom looking for a spoon in the wrong drawer. She's in a gray-polyester pantsuit, a bowl of granola on the counter, coffee steaming in the French press. My sister is at the kitchen table in her pajamas, hunched over her phone like always.

"Good morning," I say as pleasantly as possible.

"Good morning, Freya," Mom replies.

May doesn't answer. Guess she still hates me. Mom realizes she's looking in the junk drawer for a spoon and pivots to the other side of the stove. When she finds one, she holds it up like it's a gavel.

"Okay, ladies," she said, "we all had a hard day yesterday. But we are going to turn this long weekend around."

Neither of us responds. Mom sighs. "That's it. I've made an executive decision. You're both coming with me to Manhattan."

May looks up from her phone. "What? No! I have plans here."

"Well, plans change," Mom says, "and we need family time. You're going to stay at Grandma and Grandpa's while I'm at the conference. I'll drop you off. We'll stay there overnight and come back Monday morning. Maybe we can even get a nice breakfast somewhere on the way down. *Together.* With everyone speaking in full sentences."

May stands up and crosses her arms. "I literally can't go. I organized a—"

"End of discussion," Mom interrupts. She's using her scary professor voice—the one I know she adopts whenever she's telling her students that they need to start working harder. "We're leaving at nine thirty. So both of you should be packed and ready in twenty minutes."

I think my sister's head is about to explode.

"I suggest you girls go get changed," Mom says, sipping her coffee.

May scowls. She stomps toward me as she beelines for the stairs.

"This is your fault," she mutters, just out of Mom's earshot.

I knead my temples.

Fact 1: May spoke to me.

Fact 2: She didn't have anything nice to say.

Fact 3: I have to spend the next twenty-four hours with my sister.

# TEXT MESSAGES

On the car ride to Manhattan, Mom listens to a boring economics podcast while May types furiously on her phone like she's the president of the United States and she *must* update her cabinet on some top secret report. I stare out at the road and try to count the number of cell towers disguised as trees between Westchester and New York City. It'll be good to get out of Hartswood for a little bit. I left a lot of mess behind. I glance at May's profile in the front seat, long hair draped over her knees. She looks pretty when she's focused, though I'd rather jump out of a moving car than tell her that. My sister keeps typing. I fiddle with my own cell. Maybe *I* should be the one texting all my friends.

I pull down my notifications and scroll through Darley's and Billie's twenty messages again.

*Freya, are you okay?*

*Can you plz text us so we know you're ok*

*Are you mad*

*Was it Adrian*

*It was NOT Adrian, Billie*

*Well it could have been*

If my friends weren't so annoying, they'd make a great comedy act. I hover over my keyboard. It's been a weekend of truth-telling so far, so I might as well continue.

*Hi,* I write. *Sorry I didn't respond until now. I'm on my way to Manhattan to visit my grandparents. I was kinda upset by what happened in the movie so that's why I ran out. Sometimes things remind me of my dad and then I panic. I think I'm okay now.*

I bite the inside of my cheek. Should I really be saying all this? The last time Billie, Darley, and I had a *real* conversation about my dad was at the funeral, and even then, they quickly pivoted to eating Lindt truffles and gossiping about who in our grade had the biggest summer transformation.

Mom stops at a red light, and we lurch forward.

"Oops," she says sheepishly. May makes a disapproving sound.

We're in the Bronx now, stuck in traffic. Outside, on a court tucked in the corner of a small city park, three boys play basketball. They look about the age Darley,

Billie, and I were when we first met. Little second graders whose biggest worries were relay races and spelling tests. I pick at my cuticle. Darley and Billie are my best friends, and they care—at least enough to text me in the group chat even if they're clearly fighting with each other. I finish the note with *Let's hang out in the college courtyard after school on Tuesday?* and press SEND.

Two down, one to go.

Gus's last texts say, *Hey are you all right?* and *I know you told me not to enter you in the baking thing but I couldn't let your cookies go to waste. Please don't be mad at me!!! Anyway, you got third place! I'm dropping off your ribbon at your house.* I picture him writing *Freya June Sun* on the sign-up sheet in his adorably bad handwriting. I imagine him lumbering up my front porch steps with his mime shirt and weirdly lush hair. I think about his bike, probably toppled in the grass as he dashed toward my door. I think about his face when we were laughing in his kitchen, our hands covered in flour. I remember his honesty promise to me and his soothing, comforting voice. I might have been wrong about Gus Choi. I might have been really, really wrong.

I text back, *I'm doing a lot better now. You don't have to apologize for entering me in the contest. I'm really happy you did that. And thanks for bringing the ribbon over! I can't believe people liked the hup toh soh* ☺

Gus responds immediately. *Hi!! I'm glad you're feeling better and that you're not mad at me lol!! I was worried. And ya, everyone LOVED your cookies like Ms. Bethany said you should join the Great British Baking Show.*

I roll my eyes. *I'm not British*

*Golly gee, what a pity!!*

*Hahaha*

*:D*

*How'd your yaksik go?*

*Great! Everyone ate so many I didn't have any leftovers. And I got an honorable mention*

*Yay!!!*

I wish I could have seen Gus get his ribbon, too.

The car is now passing over the 145th Street Bridge across the Harlem River, and even though it's disgusting, it's a blur of sparkly blue amid the skyscrapers and bridges and ugly highway railings. I squeeze the cupholder before typing out my next message.

*Hey Gus?*

*Ya Freya?*

*I think you're kinda cool*

*That's good coz I think you're kinda cool too*

☺

May's not the only one who can get things done in a car ride.

# MAY'S PROPOSITION

Grandma and Grandpa's apartment is exactly as it always is: old, dark, and filled to the brim with dusty books. Mom's at her conference, Grandpa's in the kitchen doing a crossword and eating sliced oranges (seriously, I think they've bought out all the oranges in a twenty-block radius), and Grandma's watching the Chinese news channel (somehow, that's a cable station). I don't know why but the news in Mandarin sounds even angrier than the news in English—and the news is already pretty angry in English.

May has moved on from texting everyone she knows to pacing back and forth in the living room. I'd ask her why, but she'd probably ignore me or tell me that everything's all my fault again. Her plans at home must have been *really* excellent.

Suddenly, she stops pacing and rolls the scrunchie off her wrist, throwing her hair into a high ponytail.

"Grandma?" she asks.

"Mmm?"

My grandmother's sitting in a folding chair two feet from the television, her wire-rimmed glasses reflecting a collage of colors.

"I have a big school project due Tuesday. And I, um, have to get some supplies for it. Can I go out to the craft store? It's just, like, five blocks away."

May has a school project? She's never mentioned it before. And there's a craft store five blocks away? I didn't even know craft stores *existed* in Manhattan.

Grandma points the remote at the television and turns down the volume. Her silver glasses slide down her nose.

"I don't know, May, I don't like you walking around the city by yourself."

"I'm sixteen, Grandma."

"Yes, but you're not a city girl."

"I come here all the time. Like, I know Harlem by heart."

My grandmother leans over in her chair and waves in Grandpa's general direction. "Lǎo gōng, what do you think?"

Grandpa shrugs, his eyes still trained on the crossword.

He says something in Mandarin that May and I don't understand. My sister's eyes dart from grandparent to grandparent, her hands clasped.

"So?"

"You can go," Grandma decrees, "but you have to take Freya. Better to walk around the city in pairs. Safety in numbers, huh?"

*Oh no. I* have to roam Manhattan with May? My sister clearly feels the same way I do because she shakes her head at Grandma, her ponytail whipping back and forth.

"Freya doesn't need to come. I know where the craft store is."

"This city is not the suburbs. Safety in numbers," Grandma repeats. "Be back in an hour or I'll call your mother."

I mean, she can also call May since she has her cell phone number, but I guess the "one-hour rule" is less of a check-in time and more of a threat. For the first time today, May looks directly at me. She stalks over to the coatrack and grabs my jean jacket, tossing it on the couch where I'm sitting so it lands with a perfect *splat*.

"Come on, Freya," she grumbles. "Let's go."

# THE RED BIRDS

The craft store is *a lot* farther than five blocks. May stalks ahead of me the whole way there, glancing back to make sure I haven't disappeared since I'm her unwanted but necessary barnacle. We swerve to avoid skateboarders and e-bikers and jaywalk on side streets and watch people trickle out of restaurants and coffee shops after lunch. May's ponytail bounces in the wind—a determined, sharp weapon of sorts. Like if I ask where the craft store really is, she might slap me with that hair.

Finally, we stop in front of imposing iron gates and a long, cobblestone pathway draped by trees. *Columbia University*, I realize. We're at Mom and Dad's alma mater—where they first met and fell in love (though Mom will always note that she went to *Barnard*, not Columbia, which she insists is superior). The cobblestoned pathway is starting to fill with students in baby tees and tiny sunglasses and cool canvas tote bags that look a lot like the one May's carrying. The people start clumping together, like they're a group. A very, very large group.

"Um, May," I say, "this is not a craft store."

"Go figure," she shoots back.

She pulls out two cardboard signs from her own tote bag and hands one to me. "Just stay with me and don't get lost, okay?"

I examine the sign. It says, DON'T BE TRASH, SAVE THE EARTH in painted black letters surrounded by yellow daisies and the recycling symbol. May grabs my wrist and starts pulling me into the crowd gathered in front of the gates.

"May," I hiss, "why are we joining a college protest?"

If it's not obvious to her, it's 100 percent clear to everyone else that I am *thirteen*, not *nineteen*. I do *not* belong with college kids.

"It's a climate change protest, not a college protest," May clarifies like that's useful information, "and this is just their meeting point. We'll only go down ten blocks or so and then come back up."

"But why are we at this protest to begin with? And what about Grandma—"

May whirls around to face me, her fingers still grasping my wrist. "If you tell Grandma or Grandpa or Mom about this, I'll literally murder you. We'll be back in less than an hour, I promise."

Okay, so my sister just threatened murder, but at least she's talking to me again. I have Mother Earth to thank for that.

From the school's entrance at 116th Street, we walk down Broadway, which is blocked off from cars with wooden barriers and lined by police officers. Hundreds of students march ahead of us, a drum somewhere up ahead booming with every step. At the front, a man with a green bandana and an orange loudspeaker totters on his friend's shoulders. He screams: *What do we want?* And somehow, everyone in the protest, including my sister, knows to scream back: *Climate justice!* He yells back: *When do we want it?* And they respond: *Now!* After a few minutes, the man switches it up and literally starts singing the lyrics to "Hot in Herre" with climate change–appropriate lyrics. Everyone belts along in unison with him. As they sing, I marvel at May thrusting her sign in the air with one hand, still clutching my wrist in the other, her face bathed in sunlight.

"May," I start, "how—"

"Oh my gosh, are you May Sun from Hartswood?"

A girl with bleached hair shoved under a bucket hat screeches to a halt in the middle of the protest. She's on her tippy-toes so she can be eye level with May. We pause, too, and the crowd behind us stumbles for a moment before swerving around us. My sister squints, her hand shading her eyes.

"Yeah," she says, "who are you?"

*Um.* Did I hit my head and forget that my sister is a celebrity? Literally, *what* is going on?

"I'm Abby Hayashi," the girl with the bucket hat says excitedly. "My cousins are from Hartswood, and we've all been following your group's social media. I'm, like, *so* impressed with everything you've done for the town. Look at the crowd there!"

Abby Hayashi sticks a phone in my sister's face. We both lean over and take in her screen—a livestream of at least a hundred or so people marching on Hartswood's main street with similar climate signs and chants. The video cuts to a close-up of the front of the crowd. In the center stands a boy with a banner that says, HARTSWOOD PROTESTS CLIMATE CHANGE. His face looks like a pinched rat's. Wait a second. I *know* that pinched-rat face.

"Is that *Lucas Vanderpool*?" I shriek.

My sister releases her hand from my wrist and quickly places it over my mouth.

"Yes," she says nonchalantly, her hand still on my

mouth as I squirm beneath her. She turns to Abby. "I'm so glad the protest is going well. I'll be back up in Westchester soon to recap."

Abby doesn't seem to care that my sister is *silencing* me because she skips away to her friend group and rejoins the chanting and cheering. When she's out of sight, May takes her hand off my mouth and wipes it on the back of her jeans.

"May," I say, arms crossed, "you have to tell me what's going on. Seriously."

I plant my feet on the asphalt, refusing to move until she speaks. I wait for my sister to yell at me, but she just sighs.

"Fine." She blows her curtain bangs off her forehead. "Every year, there's a bunch of climate change protests in New York. But no one in Hartswood does anything because people don't mobilize in the 'burbs. So I started an informal group there, and we've been organizing a sister protest on the same day as the march in the city. I was supposed to lead the rally in Hartswood today, but since Mom dragged us here, I couldn't go. Lucas is leading it for me instead."

I am trying to process everything she's saying amid the bullhorns and loudspeakers and chanting. There are so many things I want to ask May, like *You really organized an entire protest on your own?* and *How many followers do you have on TikTok or whatever?*, but instead, I say, "Lucas Vanderpool cares about climate change?"

May smirks. "He cares about lots of things, Freya. He's, like, a smart guy. The Marty to my RBG."

"The what?"

"Never mind."

We rejoin the crowd and start walking again, though now we're lingering at the back. I run the palm of my hand along the cardboard's edges.

"Why are we here then?"

May shrugs. "If I can't be in Hartswood where I'm supposed to be, I figure this is the next best place."

"Why didn't you tell Mom? She might have let you stay home."

May's shoulders stiffen. "No, she wouldn't understand. She doesn't always listen to me, Freya."

And that's when it all starts clicking in my brain. The sneaking out. The random cars in our driveway. Mom and May's constant fights upstairs.

"Were you sneaking out to organize this *protest* stuff?"

"Yes," May admits, "we couldn't get it done during school or at other people's houses after school because most of our parents weren't thrilled with the way we were pushing back against our town's fossil fuel investments. But I don't care. The planet is way more important than any of that."

She talks like a councilwoman, or a president. I'm not going to lie—I'm impressed. I tentatively hold out my arm and loop it through my sister's. I glance up to see if she's going to jerk away, but she doesn't move. She lets us link.

"You know, May," I say softly (or as softly as I can considering the noise level of this protest), "you seem like a really good leader. A really good, kind of scary leader."

May grins and then readjusts her expression so she doesn't look *too* pleased with my compliment.

"Leaders *should* be scary," she declares, "or at least intimidating."

We stay linked as we continue to march down the street. At the corner of 112th and Broadway, we turn onto a side street still blocked off from traffic. May points to a bookstore with a cobalt-blue banner.

"That's where Dad asked Mom out for the first time," she says.

"Really? I didn't know that."

May nods. "Yup, Dad told me. He'd been wanting to ask her out for ages but was too nervous. They were buying textbooks, and he was so jumpy he accidentally hit her on the head with one."

"He hit her on the head with *a textbook*? Was she okay?"

My sister laughs. "Well, I dunno, Freya, Mom's kinda

loopy sometimes. Maybe she got a concussion and hasn't been the same since."

I shake my head. "All because of Dad."

"All because of Dad."

"Well, I guess he asked her out after that, and she still said yes," I muse.

"Yup," May confirms, "and the rest was history."

We both stare at the awning and then up at the blue sky overhead. I see them coming out of the clouds in slow motion: the red birds drift through the sky, their wings spread like pink-tinged fans. They look different this time. They aren't just poised at the ready, waiting for me to make the right choice. They are brilliant and beautiful and huge. They are soaring.

May's forearm tightens around mine, and I can tell she sees them, too.

"Wow," she croaks, "it's Dad."

I smile. "It's Dad."

# LATE-NIGHT TALKS

We return to Grandma and Grandpa's within the hour, just like May promised. We even make time to stop at the Columbia bookstore so May can buy some colored pencils and poster board as cover for her "school project." Grandma doesn't bat an eye. Instead, she serves us a late lunch: chicken with snow peas and rice. Grandpa shifts his newspaper over so we have room at the table, and we dig in. The snow peas are tender, the sauce light yet salty with . . . garlic and soy sauce, I think, and a flavor I can't pinpoint. I swallow a piece of chicken.

"Grandma?"

My grandmother is washing cutlery at the sink—she almost never sits and eat with us no matter how hard we try to make her.

"Yes, Freya?"

"Can you, uh, maybe one day teach me how to make this?"

Grandma flicks her head toward me in surprise. "How to make chicken with snow peas?"

"Mm-hmm."

"Of course," Grandma says. "Next time you come, I'll show you."

I squish a snow pea between my chopsticks and smile at my plate.

In the evening, Mom comes back from her midtown conference, giddy and babbling about all the great presenters and the new things she learned and the connections she made. She tosses her blazer over the arm of the couch and kicks off her heels.

"So, girls, what did you do today?"

I'm sitting on the carpet next to May, my feet tucked under my thighs. My sister is pretending to read a book for English class, but I know she's also purposefully trying not to make eye contact with our mother.

"May and I went out to the craft store for her school project," I tell Mom, "and then we just walked around and came back. It was a really nice day out."

Mom raises her eyebrows. "You two went out? *Together?*"

"Yep," I say, "we had a good time, actually. Right, May?"

May nods. "Yup. We did."

She's still staring at her book, but her eyes crinkle with gratefulness behind the pages. Mom dramatically presses a hand to her heart.

"Well," she says, "maybe I was right for once. Bringing you girls to the city was a good idea."

We watch C-dramas on Netflix for the rest of the night. Grandma and Grandpa only have two bedrooms—one for them and one for Mom (her childhood room)—so May and I have to blow up the air mattress and sleep in the living room. Our grandparents don't really have comforters—more like random knit blankets that don't cover our feet. We pick the least scratchy ones from a pile in the hallway closet.

On the air bed, I lie on my back and listen to all the sounds of the city: honking cars and trucks, ambulance sirens, garbage trucks picking up trash, and my grandparents' neighbors walking on the floorboards above our heads. It's so different from Hartswood at night, which is silent except for the occasional crickets and the hum of a lone car on the street.

I can hear May fiddling with her rings next to me, something she always does when she's thinking hard.

"Freya?" she says.

*Uh-oh.* I hope she's not back to being mad at me again. We were having such a nice day (at least for us).

"What?" I whisper.

"I just want to say . . . well, um . . ." My sister struggles to find the words. "I just want to say I'm sorry."

Did aliens replace my sister at the protest? Are we in the multiverse and I accidentally entered another dimension?

"You are?" I ask.

"Yeah." May sighs. "For, like, what I said about Dad's superstitions and stuff. I still think you shouldn't let them rule your life. But I guess I wasn't being very nice about it."

"Thanks." I bite my lip. "I'm sorry, too. I know you care about Dad. That was mean of me."

I can tell we're both thinking about the red birds we saw at the protest, about the tears in May's eyes as we watched them dip through the sky. I can't believe they found me even after I quit the viola. Maybe Dad isn't so mad at me after all.

May rolls over on her side of the air mattress. "I think you and Dad had this bond that I didn't have. With the viola and the superstitions and stuff." She slides a ring off her finger and rubs at the silver band. "You know, when Dad died, I was fighting with him and Mom all the time. More with Mom, but, you know, it wasn't great. I was and am the *problem child*. Especially in comparison to you. You're just . . . You're just so good."

I turn my face toward my sister.

"That's not true," I tell her. "First of all, I'm not *good.* I don't even like the viola."

It feels nice to say that out loud again. It hurts less.

"And second of all, you're not the *problem child.* You're literally the opposite. Watching you at the protest today, May, I mean, you were amazing. You organized this whole thing in Westchester, and you're only, like, sixteen. You *care.* You're not just a Demogorgon."

May laughs in the hazy darkness. "Do you mean a *demagogue*?"

"Sure, whatever. Anyway, I think Dad would be proud of you. I *know* he would."

"Do you mean that?" May asks.

"Uh-huh, I do. And I think Mom will be, too. You should tell her what you've been doing. If you give her time, she'll come around. And maybe don't get sent to the principal's office for a while."

May sticks out her tongue at me, but she grabs my hand and squeezes. "Okay, Freya. I'll think about it."

I squeeze back. "Okay."

We lie there, staring up at Grandma and Grandpa's cracked and puckered living room ceiling, which desperately needs a paint job.

"Freya?" May says again.

"Yeah?"

"I believe in your red birds, just so you know. I mean,

I saw them myself. But I don't think they're trying to tell you what to do."

"What are they doing then?"

"I don't know," May admits, "but I have to think they're here to support you. And us. I think they're telling you everything's gonna be okay, especially when you're having a bad time."

I never thought about it like that. But now I'm replaying every time the birds showed up. Right before my solo. When Mr. Keating wanted me to audition for the competition. When Grandma was talking about Dad's finances. When I didn't want to play. At the protest this afternoon. Maybe Dad's final goodbye to me before he left for work wasn't his last. In some way, he's been here, waving to me all along.

"The birds are like what Dad would do if he were here," I whisper. "Support us when we need it the most."

May squeezes my hand again.

"Exactly," she says. "That's exactly right, Freya."

# THE DECISION

We drive back to Hartswood on Monday morning after breakfast together at Tom's Restaurant. In the car, Mom still listens to her economics podcast, and May still texts constantly on her phone, but I don't mind. Everything is a little different now.

At school on Tuesday, I skip my pre-homeroom trip to my locker and beeline straight for Mr. Keating's office. He's waving his baton in his swivel chair, fake-conducting a song. I take a deep breath and focus on what May said about the red birds, about Dad. *He's here to support you.* I knock.

When Mr. Keating sees me, he rushes to open the door, tripping over his loafers as he greets me.

"Freya," he says, "I'm, um, I'm glad to see you."

*After that disaster on Saturday*, is the part he doesn't say aloud.

"Hi," I say, "me too." I cut to the chase. "I'm sorry about the competition. I hope I didn't embarrass you too much."

My conductor shakes his head. "It's okay, Freya. I mean . . . Well, I was a little shocked, but I wasn't angry or anything. And you're really not the first kid to run out during an audition. Can you, uh, can you tell me what's going on, though?"

He motions to a seat across from his swivel chair. I drop my backpack on the floor and dig my fingers into the vinyl. Here goes nothing.

"I've thought a lot about it, Mr. Keating, and I've decided I want to take a break from the viola. I think I've wanted to for a while . . . but I . . . I couldn't yet. So next fall, I'd like to drop orchestra."

I examine Mr. Keating's changing expressions. Is he going to yell at me? Is he going to start sobbing? But Hartswood's most dedicated conductor simply nods.

"To be honest, Freya, I'm not surprised. After what happened at the competition and all. I'll miss having you in my orchestra, of course. But I think I'll live." He cracks a smile. "I hope you'll come back to play one day. If you want to, of course."

"I'm not sure I will," I tell him just as honestly, "but you'll definitely be the first one to know if I do."

I stand up, swinging my backpack straps over my shoulders. Mr. Keating stands up, too, and we awkwardly waver in his office. Then he sticks out his hand, and I shake it.

"It was a pleasure having you in my orchestra, Freya."

"It was a pleasure being there, Mr. Keating."

I start walking toward the door. I'm halfway between his office and the lobby when I pause.

"Mr. Keating?"

"What's up, Freya?"

"I think Xena loves playing the viola," I tell him, "and she's really good at it. You should make her the section leader when I'm gone."

Mr. Keating grins. "I'll certainly take your opinion into account. Thank you."

"You're very welcome."

# BOYFRIENDS

"All right, I have a speech to give."

Darley, Billie, and I are sprawled out on the university courtyard grass, by the big tree, just like always. They both wrote back after I texted them in the car—Billie with a couple of sentences and Darley with paragraphs and many, many exclamation points.

Darley's on her knees, stray hairs from her fishtail braid swaying in the wind. "Okay," she says, "I'm—"

"You're sorry," Billie interrupts, "we know."

"Well, *you* know, but Freya doesn't." She turns to me. "Billie and I talked, and I realized that I sorta ditched you guys for Adrian. Which was really not my best decision because, as they say, *friends are forever, boys are whatever.*"

I scrunch my eyebrows. "Who says that?"

"I do," Darley asserts, "and so does the internet." She

leans forward and throws her arms around my neck. "And like I said over text, I want to be here for you no matter what. I'm sorry I was awkward and weird when you were sad about your dad. I don't want to be like that. I want you to be able to tell me stuff."

"Me too!" Billie pipes up. "You can tell me stuff, too."

I laugh, untangling myself from Darley's grip. "Okay," I say. "Thanks. That means a lot."

It does, actually. And after my *other* outburst at the movie theater, maybe I'll be better about actually telling my best friends how I feel. It's this new thing that I've recently decided Freya 2.0 is doing.

Billie chews on her lip, holding her homework folder close to her chest. "And I should be more okay with you guys having boyfriends," she says, "since that's a thing that people have."

"*Darley* has a boyfriend," I clarify. "*I* do not."

Darley sits up, her hands on her hips. "Oh, *really*? I think a certain boy who is surprisingly a great chef would beg to differ."

"Okay, what are you talking about?"

It is extremely unfortunate that my phone pings at that exact second. Billie grabs it from my hands before I have a chance to see who's texted me.

"Hiya, Freya," she reads aloud, "do you wanna grab ice cream on Friday night? Smiley face. *Heart*."

I almost tumble into the grass. "Wait, lemme see—"

Darley lurches for my phone. "*Smiley face. Heart.* Gus Choi is asking you on a date! He's basically in love!"

"Um, can I just see my—"

"Boyfriends!" Billie shouts. "See! You all have boyfriends! Which I am fine with!"

"*Freya has a boyfriend!*" Darley yells, so loudly I'm convinced Mom can hear her from the Economics Building.

They're never going to let me live this down, are they?

"Wait," Billie says, "can we still do monthly *Forbidden Treasure* nights, though? We can change it to Saturdays if that's better for everyone."

"Yes, Billie," I reply, laughing, "you can send us a calendar invite."

# VANILLA ICE CREAM

May agrees to drive me to Lucky's Ice Cream Shop on Friday night, but her good deed does not come without instructions. At a red light, she rummages through the glove compartment and pulls out a tube of lip stain.

"You don't want lip gloss because that'll make your lips sticky while you're eating ice cream," she explains, "which is gross. So lip stain is the way to go."

She tosses it onto my lap and puts her foot on the gas pedal.

I pull down the visor mirror and carefully apply the stain. It's a delicate, muted pink. It makes me feel older, like a real teenager.

"Thanks," I say.

"No problem."

We pull into Lucky's parking lot. I've never been on

a *date* before, though I don't really know if I can call this a date, like Darley and Billie insist it is. I'm wearing a tan shirtdress with tiny rainbows on it and my go-to denim jacket. May let me borrow her gold pendant necklace but said she'd kill me if I lost it. Even though she's being nice to me lately, murder is clearly still on the table.

I lift my fingers to nervously pick at my cuticles, but my sister swats my hand away.

"Don't do that," she says.

She peeks out the window, and we both see Gus leaping from his mom's car. I *really* wish May would let me pick my cuticles.

"I'll swing by in an hour," she says, peering into the depths of her purse. She emerges with her wallet and takes out a ten-dollar bill. "For that large ice-cream cone I owe you. And a little extra."

I fling my arms around May, and she pats the back of my head.

"Thanks, May."

"Have a good *date*."

"You're gross," I say, opening the car door.

"No, you are."

Lucky's is packed, since there's not much else to do in Hartswood on a Friday night other than this, the movies, and the mall. Thankfully, I don't see anyone from school that I'd rather *not* see. Gus is in line already. He waves.

His hair is perfect today, a tendril loosely hanging down the center of his forehead. I gulp.

"Hey!" Gus says, "did you get here okay?"

I play with May's necklace. "Um, it was like a five-minute drive."

"Oh, right. Same."

We step up to order. Gus gets chocolate soft serve in a cone, and I get a strawberry twist in a cup instead of my usual vanilla because I'm trying new things these days. There are tons of people at the tables with umbrellas, so we find a bench on the side of the store, away from the crowds. It feels strange sitting with Gus under no pretenses—no school projects or hallway freak-outs or grocery store trips. But after a few minutes of awkward silence, Gus starts rambling about how he wishes he could make ice cream from scratch, and I talk about my favorite ice-cream place in Florida, and sooner or later, we end up on the topic of *Forbidden Treasure*, and it's just like normal.

Before I know it, I'm finishing my last bite of strawberry-vanilla ice cream. (I chickened out and got a medium instead of a large.) I get up from the bench and throw my cup in the recycling bin. When I return, Gus is demolishing the rest of his chocolate. I giggle to myself. It reminds me of the night he spilled milkshake all over my dress.

"You know," I say, plopping back down beside him, "for a while, I didn't really like you that much."

Gus glances up from his ice cream. "Because I spilled that milkshake on you?"

"Yeah, and 'cause you ate my salami sandwich in third grade."

"I did not."

"You did, too."

Gus shakes his waves back and forth. "I swear on every edition of *Forbidden Treasure* I own that I didn't eat your salami sandwich in third grade."

"Guess you better get rid of all your editions of *Forbidden Treasure*, then."

Gus starts theatrically groaning and whining while I laugh. When we're silent again, he thoughtfully chews on his cone.

"So you didn't like me then . . . but do you like me now?"

I bite my lip so I don't smile too hard. "Maybe. Kinda. Yes." *Okay, I give up.* "Yes, Gus Choi, I like you."

Gus makes no attempt to hide *his* expression, and I think his grin might actually break his face.

"I like you, too," he whispers.

He scoots over so his leg is brushing my dress. "Could I, uhhh, kiss you? On the cheek?"

*Did the weather just get fifty times warmer or is it just me?*

"All right," I say, "as long as you don't spill your ice cream on me in the process."

"I wouldn't dare," Gus whispers.

And then he leans over, his lips smooth and lovely and wonderful on my skin. This might be the best night of seventh grade ever.

# FOR DAD

TWO MONTHS LATER

I'm standing over the counter with a bag of thick red icing in my hand. I examine my creation. I think it looks pretty decent. Mom and May are in the dining room—a place we never use except for special occasions. I can hear them laughing over takeout from Colette's. May's high-pitched cackle and the smell of burgers and gooey grilled cheeses float past the foyer and into the kitchen. I wouldn't say Mom and May are *best friends*, but they haven't argued in at least three weeks. I call that an achievement.

Spring petals have fallen, ushering in the heat of full summer—pool parties, no homework, day camps (a cooking course for me), internships (May travels to the city every week to intern at the American Civil Liberties Union, aka the ACLU), and Mom's family-dictated grief counseling, where I talk about Dad a lot, even when it hurts. On warm evenings, Gus and I get ice cream and ride our bikes around the neighborhood. I spend my weekends with Darley and Billie, eating popcorn and watching bad rom-coms and wondering what eighth grade will be like.

I shiver. I'm not ready to be an *eighth grader* yet. I still have a month and a half left.

My sister traipses into the kitchen, a jaw clip between her teeth as she rolls her hair into a loose bun.

"Wow, Freya," she says, admiring the spread on the counter, "you've outdone yourself. It's a good thing I saved room for dessert."

"Thanks," I reply.

May moves to stand next to me, her dangly jade earrings swaying as she walks. She pats the back of my head like I'm her pet, but I don't mind it too much. It's kind of nice.

"I can't believe you did all this yourself," she continues. "You're going to have to make dessert for all my environmental club meetings next year."

"You're going to have to pay me in ice cream forever if you want that," I retort.

May scrunches her nose. "You strike a hard bargain, but I appreciate a tough negotiator."

She's right, though. Not about baking for all her

environmental club friends (she actually hosts most meetings at our house with Mom's permission—shocker, I know), but about the *doing it all myself.* Gus offered to help countless times. But I told him this was something *I* had to handle. On my own.

I bend down so I'm eye level with the crimson-red icing and inspect it again. Yes, it's perfect.

May carries out the first set of dishes to the dining room while I handle the main event. We file in, Mom's face aglow under the dining room chandelier as she surveys my treats.

Hup toh soh. Egg tarts. Lotus seed buns. And, in my hands, a buttercream-frosted vanilla cake with two red birds iced onto its center.

"Oh, Freya," Mom exclaims, "this is wonderful."

"It's all of Dad's favorite treats," I tell her, though I'm positive she already knows.

"He would have loved this," Mom replies, whipping out her phone to take photos.

I balance the cake tray in my hands, my shadow casting curved lines across the iced birds' bodies. I wonder if the real pair of red birds are out there—soaring around New York, ready to appear when we need them the most. I hope they know how much they mean to me. How much they mean to all of us.

May arranges the pastries so there's a spot for the cake on the center of the tablecloth.

"Happy birthday, Dad," she says.

I gently place the cake on the table, one end at a time.

"Happy birthday, Dad," I echo. My hands hover under the tray.

And then I let go.

# AUTHOR'S NOTE

For years, I've wanted to write a story about grief and a girl like Freya but couldn't find the words until now. When I was about Freya's age, my dad passed away suddenly. In an instant, the world as I knew it changed forever. Every day, I used to wake up for school and stumble down to the kitchen, where my dad and I would silently share the morning newspaper—he'd read the actual news and I'd read the comics. He was at every concert, standing and singing along to every Hallelujah Chorus, cheering in the stands for all my extracurriculars (from softball to figure skating to musical theater), telling me tall tales over dinner, and cuddling with me on the couch before I went to sleep.

I miss him. And more than a decade later, I mourn the fact that he won't get to see the person I've become. It's scary losing a loved one and then forging a new path for yourself—not knowing whether that loved one will approve, or be proud, or be disappointed, or simply be overjoyed. I had to accept the grief, the loss, the not knowing and form my opinions, be my own person. Just like Freya. Just like anyone reading this who has lost a loved one, especially at a young age.

And to you, I say: I'm proud of you for pushing on. Like Freya's red birds, I hope you continue to soar.

# HUP TOH SOH

*Learn how to make hup toh soh like Freya!*

INGREDIENTS

- 2 cups flour
- ½ teaspoon baking soda
- ¼ teaspoon baking powder
- 8 tablespoons butter at room temperature
- ½ cup sugar
- ¼ teaspoon salt
- ¾ chopped walnuts, plus 12 whole walnut halves
- 1 egg

STEP 1:

Preheat the oven to 350 degrees Fahrenheit.

STEP 2:

In a medium-size bowl, combine the flour, baking soda,

and baking powder. In a separate, larger bowl, mix together the butter, sugar, and salt, and stir until you can't see any butter chunks and the mixture is creamy. Slowly pour the flour, baking soda, and baking powder into the butter mixture. Add the chopped walnuts.

STEP 3:

In a separate bowl, whisk the egg until lightly bubbly. Scoop out two tablespoons of egg and set aside. Pour the rest of the egg into the dough mixture. Using your hands, knead the mixture until it forms a ball.

STEP 4:

Line a baking sheet with parchment paper. Split the dough ball into twelve equal pieces. Roll each piece into a ball and then place the cookies on the baking sheet, a couple inches apart.

STEP 5:

Press the whole walnut halves carefully and gently into each cookie. Brush each cookie with the leftover tablespoons of egg. Bake for twenty minutes, or until golden brown. Wait until they cool and then eat and enjoy!

*Inspired by The Woks of Life's Chinese Walnut Cookies recipe.*

# DEEP-DISH CHOCOLATE CHIP COOKIE

*Make Freya's famous deep-dish chocolate chip cookie.*

INGREDIENTS

- 2 sticks butter
- 1 cup granulated sugar
- ½ cup brown sugar, packed
- 2 teaspoons vanilla
- 2 tablespoons maple syrup
- 2 eggs
- 1½ cups flour
- 1 teaspoon baking soda
- ½ teaspoon salt
- 1 cup chocolate chunks (pro tip: grab your favorite giant chocolate bar and slice it up into small pieces)
- ½ cup chocolate chips

¼ cup of chocolate (either chocolate chunks or chocolate chips)
A dash of sea salt

STEP 1:
Preheat the oven to 350 degrees Fahrenheit.

STEP 2:
Microwave the butter for 45 seconds to one minute until it's lightly melted.

STEP 3:
In a large mixing bowl, combine butter and sugars with a whisk or an electric mixer on low speed. Add vanilla, maple syrup, and eggs, and mix together until smooth. Finally, slowly add the flour, baking soda, and salt and combine until a smooth dough forms.

STEP 4:
Pour in the chocolate chunks and chocolate chips (*not* the ¼ cup of chocolate—we'll use that for later!) and mix together until fully combined.

STEP 5:
Line a large cast-iron skillet with parchment paper, and using the back of a mixing spoon or spatula, press the

dough mixture into the pan until the dough touches every side.

STEP 6:

Bake for 20–25 minutes, or until the top of the cookie is golden brown.

STEP 7:

Remove the cookie skillet from the oven (be careful!) and let cool. Microwave the ¼ cup of chocolate in 15- to 20-second increments until creamy and smooth. Using a spoon or fork, drizzle the melted chocolate across the top of the cookie. Sprinkle a dash of sea salt on top. Serve and enjoy!

*Inspired by Pinch of Yum's Deep-Dish Chocolate Chip Cookie with Caramel and Sea Salt recipe.*

# ACKNOWLEDGMENTS

I am indebted to everyone who helped me unearth the words to this story:

Wes Adams, who casually asked me if I was interested in writing novels so many moons ago and truly changed my life. Thank you for your insight, creativity, and keen eye.

Marietta Zacker, the wisest agent in all the land, I owe you a hundred deep-dish chocolate chip cookies.

Thank you to everyone at Farrar Straus Giroux Books for Young Readers and Macmillan Children's Group, including Hannah Miller, for your perceptive edits; Aurora Parlagreco, for your impeccable design; Morgan Rath, for pushing *Maybe It's a Sign* out to more readers; and Karin Kipp, Mindy Fichter, and Allyson Floridia, for your attention to detail.

Sher Rill Ng, thank you for your absolutely gorgeous illustrations.

And a shout-out to my Writers' Club friends who saw the very first iteration of this story and cheered me on to the finish line.

Jack, there are no thank-yous in the world that would suffice, but know that I am grateful for your listening ear, your positivity, your patience, your kindness, and your love. The Gus to my Freya, foreverrrrr.

And to my family—Mom, Diana, and Grandma—we have weathered every storm together, and I am so proud for the ways we have carried on. Thank you for lifting me up every step of the way, in writing and in life. I love you so much.

This is for you, Dad: who unabashedly taped all my stories and essays on your office door, who came to every concert, who stood for every Hallelujah Chorus, who supported every dream and passion of mine. Your love puts me at the top of the world.